MW00851024

A Very Irish Christmas

THE GREATEST
IRISH HOLIDAY STORIES
OF ALL TIME

NEW VESSEL PRESS
NEW YORK

Cover design by Ashling Lindsay
Book design by Beth Steidle
Saint Agnes typeface © Great Lakes Lettering (www.GreatLakesLettering.com)

Library of Congress Cataloging-in-Publication Data
Various
A Very Irish Christmas: The Greatest Irish Holiday Stories of All Time / various authors.
p. cm.
ISBN 978-1-939931-96-2
Library of Congress Control Number 2021935181
Ireland—Fiction

Table of Contents

A Very Irish Christmas

The Wexford Carol

Good people all, this Christmas time,
Consider well and bear in mind
What our good God for us has done
In sending his beloved son
With Mary holy we should pray,
To God with love this Christmas Day
In Bethlehem upon that morn,
There was a blessed Messiah born

The night before that happy tide
The noble Virgin and her guide
Were long time seeking up and down
To find a lodging in the town
But mark right well what came to pass
From every door repelled, alas
As was foretold, their refuge all
Was but a humble ox's stall

Near Bethlehem did shepherds keep
Their flocks of lambs and feeding sheep
To whom God's angel did appear

Which put the shepherds in great fear
Arise and go, the angels said
To Bethlehem, be not afraid
For there you'll find, this happy morn
A princely babe, sweet Jesus, born

With thankful heart and joyful mind
The shepherds went the babe to find
And as God's angel had foretold
They did our Saviour Christ behold
Within a manger he was laid
And by his side a virgin maid
Attending on the Lord of Life
Who came on earth to end all strife

There were three wise men from afar
Directed by a glorious star
And on they wandered night and day
Until they came where Jesus lay
And when they came unto that place
Where our beloved Messiah lay
They humbly cast them at his feet
With gifts of gold and incense sweet.

Shopping for Christmas Dinner

ANNE ENRIGHT

ROSALEEN TOLD CONSTANCE SHE DID not want a present this year. She said it in a faint voice, meaning she would be dead soon so what was the point? What was an object—when you would not have it for long? Too much? Not enough? It was hard to say.

Constance thought she was immune to this sort of guff, but she also needed to tell her mother that she was not about to die so she went up to Galway and trawled through every last thing in the shops, until she found a thick silk scarf that was the same price as a new microwave and so beautiful you could not say what colour it was, except there was lilac in there and also pearl, all of which would be perfect for her mother's complexion and for her silver-white hair.

"Oh I can't remember," she would say when her mother asked the price, or complained about the price. Times were good. Constance bought a wheel of Camembert, various boxes of chocolates, Parma ham and beautiful, small grapes that were more yellow than green. She got her hair done in a place so posh it didn't look done at all. Then she drove back home through the winter darkness in the smell of PVC and ripening cheese, happy in her car. Constance loved to drive. It was the perfect excuse. For what, she did not know. But there was such simplicity to it: crossing great distances to stop an inch away from the kerb, opening the door.

The next morning she was back behind the wheel, picking Dan up from the airport, depositing him at her mother's, back in to the butcher's and a few things around town, a poinsettia for the cleaner, a trio of hyacinths for the cleaner's mother who was in hospital in Limerick and could not understand a thing the doctors told her. The cleaner was from Mongolia, a fact that made Constance slightly dizzy. But it was just true. Her cleaner—good-hearted, a little bit vague with a duster—was from Ulan Bator. Constance left the presents with her money on the kitchen table, then back out to Ardeevin with the turkey and a quick tidy up while she was there: checking supplies, running a Hoover, though her mother hated the sound of the Hoover. After which, home to drive Shauna to a pal's house, her fake tan leaving a shadow on the cream upholstery of the Lexus.

"Ooofff," said Constance, when she saw it and then chastised her temper. That all her problems should be so small.

The next morning, she went early into Ennis. It was 10 a.m. on Christmas Eve and the supermarket was like the Apocalypse, people grabbing without looking, and things fallen in the aisles. But there was no good time to do this, you just had to get through it. Constance pushed her trolley to the vegetable section: celery, carrots, parsnips for Dessie, who liked them. Sausage and sage for the stuffing, an experimental bag of chestnuts, vacuum-packed. Constance bought a case of Prosecco on special offer to wrap and leave on various doorsteps and threw in eight frozen pizzas in case the kids rolled up with friends. Frozen berries. Different ice cream. She got wine, sherry, whiskey, fresh nuts, salted nuts, crisps, bags and bags of apples, two mangoes, a melon, dark cherries for the fruit salad, root ginger, fresh mint, a wooden crate of satsumas, the fruit cold and promising sweet, each one with its own sprig of green dark leaves. She got wrapping paper, red paper napkins, Sellotape, and—more out of habit, now the children were grown—packs and packs of batteries, triple A, double A, a few Cs. She took five squat candles in cream-coloured beeswax to fill the cracked hearth in the good room at Ardeevin, where no fire was lit this ten years past, and two long rolls of simple red baubles to fill the gaps on her mother's tree. She went back for more sausages because she had forgotten about breakfast. Tomatoes. Bacon. Eggs. She went back to the dairy section for more cheese. Back to the fruit aisle for seedless grapes. Back to the biscuit aisle for water biscuits. She searched high and low for string to keep the cloth on the pudding, stopped at the delicatessen counter for pesto, chicken liver pâté, tubs of olives. She got some ready-cooked drumsticks to keep people going. At every corner, she met a neighbour, an old friend, they rolled their eyes and threw Christmas greetings, and no one thought her rude for not stopping to converse. She smiled at a baby in the queue for the till.

"I know!" she said. "Yes I know!" The baby considered her fully. The baby gave her a look that was complete.

"Yes!" she said again, and got the curl of a sweet, thoughtful smile.

All this kept Constance occupied until the time came to unload the contents of her trolley onto the conveyor. The baby held itself so proudly erect, the young mother underneath it looked like a prop. She looked like some kind of clapped-out baby stand.

"You're doing great," Constance told her. "You're doing a great job."

The bill came to four hundred and ten euros, a new record. She thought she should keep the receipt for posterity. Dessie would be almost proud.

Constance pushed her trolley onto the walkway and the wheels locked cleverly on to the metal beneath them, and she was happy happy happy, as she sank towards the car park. She thanked God from the burning, rising depth of herself for this unexpected life—a man who loved her, two sons taller than their father, and a daughter who kissed her still when no one was there to see. She could not believe this was the way things had turned out.

Her feet were swollen already; she could feel them throb, hot in the wrong shoes. Constance bumped the trolley off the walkway, set her trotters thumping across the concrete of the car park. It was half past eleven on Christmas Eve. In the pocket of her coat, her phone started to ring and, by the telepathy of the timing, Constance knew it was her mother.

"What is it, darling?" she said, remembering, as she did so, that she had forgotten the Brussels sprouts.

"He's still asleep," said Rosaleen. For a moment Constance thought she was talking about her father, a man who was not asleep, but dead.

"Well don't wake him," she said.

Dan. Of course, she meant Dan, who was jet-lagged.

"Should I?"

"Or maybe do. Yeah. Get him straightened out."

There was a pause from Rosaleen. *Straightened out.*

"You think?"

"Have you everything?" said Constance.

"I don't know," said her mother.

"Don't worry."

"It's a lot of work," Rosaleen said, with a real despair in her voice; you would think she had just spent an hour in the insanity of the supermarket, not Constance.

"But I suppose it's worth it to have you all here."

"I suppose."

"I'll be sorry to see it go." She was talking about the house again. Anytime she felt needy now, or lost or uncertain, she talked about the house.

"Right," said Constance. "Listen, Mammy."

"Mammy," said Rosaleen.

"Listen—"

"Oh, don't bother. I'll let you go." And she was gone.

It was Rosaleen, of course, who wanted Brussels sprouts, no one else ate them. Constance stood for a moment, blank behind the crammed boot of the Lexus. You can't have Christmas without Brussels sprouts.

Sometimes even Rosaleen left them on her plate. Something to do with cruciferous vegetables, or nightshades, because even vegetables were poison to her when the wind was from the north-east.

"Oh what the hell," said Constance. She slammed the boot shut and turned her sore feet back to the walkway and the horrors of the vegetable section. Then over to the spices to get nutmeg, which was the way Rosaleen liked her Brussels, with unsalted butter. And it was a good thing she went back up, because she had no cranberry sauce either—unbelievably—no brandy for the brandy butter, no honey to glaze the ham. It was as though she had thrown the whole shop in the trolley and bought nothing. She had no big foil for the turkey. Constance grabbed some potato salad, coleslaw, smoked salmon, mayonnaise, more tomatoes, litre bottles of fizzy drinks for the kids, kitchen roll, cling film, extra toilet paper, extra bin bags. She didn't even look at the bill after another fifteen minutes in the queue behind some woman who had forgotten flowers—as she announced—and abandoned her groceries to get them, after which Constance did exactly the same thing, fetching two bouquets of strong pink lilies because they had no white left. She was on the road home before she remembered potatoes, thought about pulling over to the side of the road and digging some out of a field, imagined herself with her hands in the earth, scrabbling around for a few spuds.

Lifting her head to howl.

Back in Aughavanna she unpacked and sorted the stuff that would go over to Ardeevin for the Christmas dinner and she repacked that. Then she went to Rory's room, where the child was sleeping off a hangover. Constance took off her shoes and climbed on to the bed behind him.

"Oh fuck," he said.

"Your own fault," said his mother, as she spooned into him, with the duvet between them and the wall at her back.

"Ah, Ma," he said and flapped a big hand over his shoulder to find a bit of her, which happened to be the top of her head. But Rory was always easy to hold; easy to carry and easy to kiss, and there, in the smell of last night's beer and his rude good health, fretful, lumpy Constance McGrath fell asleep.

In the evening she brought Shauna over to Ardeevin with the ingredients for the stuffing and they put it all together right there at the table in the big kitchen. Dan knew exactly what to do with the experimental bag of chestnuts. They chopped and diced, the three of them, while the others were at the pub, and they put the vegetables underwater for the next day while Rosaleen supervised happily from the chair by the range. Dan talked about Tim Burton with Shauna and they discussed the veins on Madonna's arms. He asked a couple of excruciating questions about pop music; she asked about an artist called Cindy Sherman, and this just knocked Dan for six. He kissed the child before they left; he piled her hair on the top of her head, saying, "Look at you!" and Constance would have loved to stay longer, to be that thing, a grown-up child in her parents' house, but she had presents to wrap back in Aughavanna and she did not get to bed, as it turned out, until after two.

Frank Forrest's Mince Pie

CANON PATRICK AUGUSTINE SHEEHAN

"I DECLARE, FRANK," SAID MRS. Forrest, "that is the fourth mince pie you have eaten this evening. I am afraid, my boy, they will make you ill, so put away this one until tomorrow."

Frank knew not how to disobey his beloved mother, so he promptly took up the delicacy and placed it in the cupboard. It was Christmas Eve. Presently a feeble, timid knock was heard; and, as cook was ever so busy preparing tarts and pies for the morrow, Frank ran to the door and opened it. A gust of sleety wind nearly lifted him from his feet, and a few snowflakes fell softly on the floor, and melted slowly on the carpet in the hall.

"Something for the children," said a weak, faltering voice; and Frank saw before him a pale, delicate woman shivering in the icy wind. She had a child in her arms, looking sickly, and the snow had made a little crown for his head on the cloak which his mother had wrapped around him. She held another child by the hand, and its little rags flapped and fluttered, as the cruel storm tossed them, and pierced the little limbs with its icy needles.

"Stop a moment," said Frank, who was a rough, brusque, manly lad, but had tender feelings, though he was unconscious of possessing them. In a few moments he returned with the following miscellany, several buns, scraps of cold meat, a paper of tea, a paper of soft sugar, a bunch of raisins, a wooden monkey on a stick, a battered doll, and, crowning all, his own mince pie, which he had put away for the morrow.

"God bless you, dear," said the woman, as she opened her apron and wrapped up all these treasures; and a smile flashed across her face and lighted up her eyes, as if an angel had rushed by and touched and transfigured her.

Nine o'clock came, and Frank sat by his bedroom fire, watching the flames dancing and leaping, and gambolling around the bars. Then, slowly and reluctantly, he pulled off one shoe after another, and soon found himself nestling in his little cot, listening to the wild storm that shook the windows, and wondering where were the children resting whom he had seen that afternoon. Softly sleep stole upon him, and he closed his eyes in the peaceful slumber of boyhood.

Boom—boom—boom. It was the great cathedral bell swinging out the midnight hour, and sending its welcome tones on the wings of the storm. Frank started up.

Ding-dong, ding-dong, ding-dong; and mingling their sweet silvery notes with the deep booming, the joybells pealed out rapturously the Christmas chimes. Frank heard the hall door open and shut, and he knew that mother was going through the storm to the Midnight Mass. He rubbed his eyes, and looked around. Heigho! What's this? He rubbed his eyes again, then started up and leaned on his elbow. No doubt about it. There, in his own chair, opposite the fire, was a little old man, not a bit bigger than Frank himself. He held his hands before the fire, and Frank could see their dark shadows distinctly before the red embers. For a moment the boy was astonished, but presently the boyish daring and courage came back, and he shouted cheerily:

"Hallo, old fellow, a happy Christmas!"

The stranger rose slowly, then came to the bedside, his two hands folded behind his back, and bending over the boy, he exclaimed, half-seriously, half-jestingly:

"Ah! You bad boy!"

"I am not a bad boy," said Frank, indignant at such an answer to his welcome, "and you have no right to say so."

"Where's my mince pie?" said the old man, lifting up one finger, and shaking it warningly.

"I am sure," said Frank, "I don't know where's your mince pie; but I gave mine to a poor woman."

"Ah! You bad boy," said the stranger again, as he slowly turned away and took up his seat by the fireplace.

But Frank knew that the old man did not mean what he said. Presently, his hand dived deep, deep down into his pocket, and he placed on the table, near Frank's collar and cuffs, the very identical mince pie that Frank had given the poor woman at the door. There it was, with its mitred edge, its brown crust, and the five currants which Frank had ordered the cook to place crosswise on the top. The old man lifted off the crust and placed it gently beside him.

"He's going to eat it, the old glutton," thought Frank, "he surely stole it from the poor woman." But no! He simply lighted a match on the coals, and swiftly passed it round the edge of the pie before him. A bright blue flame shot upwards, flickering and flashing in the darkness till it reached the ceiling. Then it assumed gradually the form of a house on fire. The windows were shown clearly against the dark walls by the terrible flames within, and Frank could see the little spurts of fire that broke from the slates on the roof. Now there was a rumbling and the confused murmur of many voices, and the tramping of many feet, and a noise like the roaring of the sea. Then there was a wild shout, and a tiny jet of water rose like a thread from the crowd and scattered its showers upon the fire. Another shout, and the boy's heart sank within him as he saw at the window of the burning house a young lad like himself, clad only in his nightdress, terror and agony on his face, and his arms flung wildly hither and thither. A cheer went up, and a ladder was planted firmly against the window, and a sailor lad swiftly ascended, and in a moment the little fluttering figure was grasped in the strong arms, and carried safely where gentle hands and warm hearts would protect him. Frank's heart was throbbing wildly, the perspiration stood out in beads on his forehead, when he heard the harsh voice of the old man:

"Shut your eyes!"

Frank shut them, but kept one little corner open, and he saw the old man quietly taking up the crust and place it in the pie, completely extinguishing this awful conflagration. And the Christmas bells were chiming.

"Shut your eyes!" said the old man again, quite angrily. And Frank shut them and kept them closed for a long time, as he thought.

"Look," said the same voice.

Frank opened his eyes, fearing and wondering what new strange vision was going to burst on him. It was nothing terrible, but somehow the mince pie had expanded and grown into a deep and broad valley, with rugged rocks and strange dark places, and black mountains huddled together, and tossed about as if by an earthquake. And from their midst rose a mighty peak, the base of which was clothed with fir trees, and farther up were black frowning rocks, and the top was crowned by a pinnacle of snow that shot up high into the air, and was lost beyond the ceiling of the little bedroom. At the base of the mountain was a village, and there was a bustle in the village, and the noise of many tongues. In the street many mules were standing, laden with provisions, and three guides, tall and strong, and brown, strolled up and down, their alpenstocks in their hands, and huge coils of rope strung across their shoulders. Three young gentlemen stood apart, talking earnestly. They were young, scarcely more than boys, but there was vigour and courage in their looks, and gait and manner. They had not heard of the word "Danger!" At last one separated from the rest, and walked away quite dejected and angry. The word was given, and the two gentlemen and their guides set out to scale the mountain. They were watched until they turned the spur of the hill. Then one ringing cheer, and they disappeared in the shadows of the mountains. The day wore on, and evening came. But before the twilight descended, Frank saw that people came from their houses with long telescopes, and levelled them at the snowy summit. Nothing was visible there, as Frank could see, but the cold, hard, glittering snow, shining pink and ruby from the reflections of the fire. Suddenly there was a shout: "There they are!" Frank looked, and thought he saw five tiny black specks in the snow, linked together by a thread. Slowly these specks moved up the slippery surface until they were lost in the clouds. A few minutes later those same black specks reappeared, toiling down the steep side of the mountain of ice. Frank held his breath. They had already travelled down half the mountain, when the lowest figure on the rope fell, and one after another the brave climbers were tossed from cliff to cliff, from precipice to precipice, until they were lost in the black valleys beneath. A cry of horror had gone up from the village. Frank shut his eyes, and put his fingers in his ears. After a few moments he looked again, and saw lights flashing in the village, and dark figures hurrying to and fro, and he felt they were going out to seek for the dead bodies of the guides and the two gentlemen. Presently a bell began to toll, and Frank thought it too cheerful for a funeral; for now down the slope of the hill, in amongst the trees, out across the valley, he saw the lights shining, and slowly the procession entered the village. Mountaineers, with their heads bent down, carried on their shoulders a bier, and on the bier was something covered with a black cloth. Behind them came a young man, whom Frank recognised as the companion, who was left behind in the morning. He was weeping silently, now and again passing his handkerchief across his face.

For one moment he raised his head, and the red light of the torches fell upon him, and Frank saw that it was himself, and he felt himself choking at the thought of his narrow escape from a terrible death. He lay for a while thinking and thinking, when once more he saw the old man by the fire with the mince pie on the table, but the vision of the valley was gone. But the Christmas chimes were ringing.

After a little while, once more the voice of the old man, now very gently and lovingly, said, "Shut your eyes!" Frank closed his eyes sorrowfully, for he felt very sad and frightened, and he dreaded another terrible picture.

"Now," said the old man, "you may look!"

II

Timidly enough, Frank peered forth; but how his heart bounded with joy when he saw his own beautiful harbour painted in its richest colourings of blue and gold, the sunshine streaming over its surface, and the little waves dancing and leaping and flashing. He looked for a long time out over the waters, but he heard the noise of laughter and talking quite close at hand, and he saw just beneath him a large, beautiful boat, and somehow he thought that this boat was but his mince pie lengthened out and decorated. It was heaving and rocking on the water, and it had the straightest mast and the whitest sail in the world. And in the stern Frank saw quite a crowd of "fair women and brave men," and he knew them all as the friends of his boyhood, though they were changed. Stout watermen in blue jerseys were lifting hampers over the gunwale, and over all there was a something Frank never saw before. It was a joy and a peace and a glory as if reflected from some light brighter than the sunshine. But he himself was very sad. And they pitied him, and said, "Another time, Frank; don't grieve too much." And then the oars were planted firmly on the gravel, and the boat was pushed away, and after a few strokes the sail was lifted, and the breeze caught it and carried the gay barque like a bird over the bright waters. Frank turned away sick and disappointed, but lo! as he came along from the Admiralty Pier, he saw facing him the poor woman whom he had relieved and her children. But she was changed. She had on that strange look which passed across her face when the angel touched her, and her child was bright and ruddy, and held forth his hands to Frank, and the little girl, dressed ever so beautifully, caught Frank and bent him down towards her, and whispered something that Frank could not hear. But a strange peace stole over his heart, and all the sorrow and disappointment were gone.

But when the evening came and the lamp was lighted, and the books were opened, the same sadness stole into his heart. Suddenly there was a sharp ring, and a succession of knocks, and hurried whisperings at the door, and he heard his mother's voice saying, "My God!" and then the door of his room opened, and his mother glided in, and her face was wet with tears, and Frank knew that the gay barque of the morning was drifting out a sad wreck into the high seas, and he knew also that his dear friends from whom he had parted so sadly in the morning were now lying cold and still on the sand and shingle down deep beneath the cold blue waters. But mother came near him, and flung her arms round him, and he heard her say:

"Why, Frank, you lazy boy, still in bed at eight o'clock Christmas morning. You promised to be first in the sacristy to bid Father Ambrose a happy Christmas; and now you must wait for High Mass, and there's a pile of Christmas Cards waiting for you."

Frank lay still a moment, collecting his thoughts, doubting all things, thinking all things a dream. But there was the white light of the Christmas snow shining in his room, and there was the bell ringing for Mass, and drawing a long sigh, he exclaimed:

"Oh mother, I had such a dream."

"Never mind, my boy," said his mother; "you can tell it by and by!"

And by and by, when the tables were cleared and they were sitting round the fire, and there was not a shadow of gloom on the gay little circle, Frank told his dream, his hand softly clasped by his mother. And when he had done, she smoothed away his fair locks from his forehead, and kissed him gently, and said:

"It was not a dream, Frank, but a vision of dangers from which the good God will preserve my boy for his kindness to the little ones of Christ."

Whimsical Beasts

AISLING MAGUIRE

HE KEPT HER ON THE outskirts of the city in a flat fifteen floors up from the ground. Here he had given rein to every whim of his fantasy, masking the blind concrete walls with swags of red crepe so that it was impossible at night to tell where the doors and windows stood. He was terrified of losing her. He had happened upon her and, indeed, could even believe that he had created her.

She was nervous, shrinking always just a little from his kiss. That charmed him, her fretful reluctance to be possessed opening at length to a languorous unfolding of herself. She regarded him with implacable eyes and never spoke until he had spoken. She would take his coat, shake out the rain and hang it behind the door, and, once he was seated, she would remove his shoes and socks to chafe his cold, tired feet between her hands and lay her cheeks first on one, then on the other.

Still, he could not believe that she was there for him, no matter what time of the evening or the day he called. At the start, in his anxiety, he kept irregular hours, returning in the middle of the morning or at lunchtime. Sometimes he would leave the flat, go downstairs, wait half an hour, and go back up; yet he found her always there, seated by the window, maybe, staring out across the gaseous yellow sky of the city. If not there, she might be lying on the black platform bed that rose on a single strut in the comer of the room like an outlandish fungus sprung from nowhere in the dead of night, or like an aerial sensitive to the atmosphere of the room and the fluctuation of their moods. Satisfied that she had composed herself to wait for him alone, he would leave again, the fast beat of his heart slackening down to an empty pace.

What she did while she was there during the day was a matter of indifference to him. He sensed, however, that her mind was not one which required great stimulation. The few newspapers that he brought home she would remove from his coat pocket, spread on the floor and, sitting cross-legged, with her elbows on her knees, and her jowls pressed into the palms of her hands, she would gaze unmoving at the pages. For a few evenings he watched her do this and, occasionally, with one finger trace the contour of the faces in the photographs, until it occurred to him that, perhaps, she could not read. She looked at him, half-smiling when he asked her and shook her head.

The letters on those pages, he thought, must appear as alien to her as the characters of Cyrillic or Arabic script to me. He was pleased that she could not read for it set a further obstacle in the path of her potential escape.

"What does it look like to you, all that writing?" he asked.

For a moment she deliberated, pulling at a twist of hair that fell to the nape of her neck, then grinned. "Like millions of tiny insects marching up and down in rows," she replied, and imitated the walk of a spider with her fingers on the page.

It was when he took up smoking again that he discovered her one peculiar habit or talent, he was not sure which it should be called, for her fingers worked with such alacrity that their movement seemed completely unwilled like the reflexive spasms of palsy. An accumulation of small gold animals proceeded from this incessant fidgeting. As soon as a packet of cigarettes had been discarded she would pounce and, with her finger and thumb slide the gold foil from the box. He thought at first that she was going to make a mock goblet plugged at the base with moistened whitepaper so that by a quick upswing of the wrist it could adhere to the ceiling, like those that stud the stained plaster of countless pubs. Had she done that he would have been disgusted and enraged, the sight of an object so useless and vulgar, repulsive to his taste. Contrary to this, he was enchanted by her creative knack, as she presented him with a golden peacock in full display.

Each evening a new specimen was added to the collection until she was pushed at last to invent new subspecies, with the features of various animals assembled in comical or grotesque shapes that recalled ancient hieroglyphs. As the dark nights of winter descended he found himself to be more and more beguiled by the glow that shone, in the reflected light of the gas stove, from this fanciful troop. She could spend hours stretched on the floor shifting the tiny creatures in an intricate choreography and her narrow greenish eyes as she stared into the pattern of movements gave back greenish flecks of golden light. Only when he might stroke her hair or touch her cheeks would she advert again to his presence and then she would reach up, take his hand, open it, and place one creature from her fragile menagerie on his palm. He accepted them as tokens of her feeling for him and when night had finally come and the lights were turned out he felt her in his arms become a miraculous exotic beast.

That she should have an artistic flair gratified him, for it seemed to redound to his credit that he should have isolated her out of the drift of vagabonds that ranged the streets. He was even moved to think that he would like to take her out, and parade her on his arm down the avenues as a man of property might do, but was brought up short by the fear that she might then expect this promenade to become a regular part of their affair. He was unwilling to disrupt the singular calm they had achieved in their fifteenth floor rooms. Besides, there was the problem of clothes; he would have to dress her in the costume of the rich and, for himself, would have to find a tailor-made suit with knife edge creases, and replace his inelegant grey coat with one of camelhair or vicuña.

No, it was better to remain aloft, balanced above the city in their crow's nest, and improvise the forests and boulevards of the world in the interlocked shafts and hollows of their limbs. Instead of taking her out he brought her a gift. The parcel contained four miniature oriental screens he had spied one morning in the corner of an antique shop window. Each one was made of a piece of outstretched silk held in a black wooden frame standing on scroll-shaped feet. The brilliance of their primary colours attracted him, the red, the blue, the yellow and the green, as bright as jewels that flashed under the passage of light. She laughed when she saw them, and placed them in a line on the windowsill just to watch the tints leap and change like the shudder of colour on a bird's feathers.

Soon the screens were incorporated into the manoeuvres of the golden menagerie, and comprised a backdrop of flats as in theatrical scenery. The movements of the animals now took on a narrative form as their comings and goings in front of and around the screens followed the routines of coincidence and conflict intrinsic to the oldest plots of all.

He wondered how far her range would extend and, in consequence, smoked more than he craved and certainly more than was healthy but there was no limit to the procession of creatures that issued from her hands. Birds and beasts of unimaginable aspect, crowned with horns, or flowering with layered wings, her multiple variations on the order of nature baffled him. Unmindful of it himself, he was becoming physically derelict in the service of her art. He was aware of bouts of coughing that shook his lungs till warm phlegm curdled at the back of his mouth. His pallor, he knew, had waned from a moderate ruddiness to a feeble grey. This much the people at the garment factory where he worked had told him, remarking with meaningless concern on the decline in his complexion; but he was dismissive, attributing any alteration in his person to the onset of winter. The deposit of nicotine in his lungs consumed his energy and the new slowness of his movements interposed a veil of hesitancy between himself and his mistress.

Then, one evening, she surprised him with a request for a child. He halted in the act of drawing the red curtain and kept his eyes bent to the city which, in the amorphous gathering of dusk was condensed to the shape of a massive engine, ignited here and there by the sodium glow of the streetlamps.

"So, this is what it comes to," he thought and recognised that the plethora of whimsical animal figures had been an elaborate prelude to this ingenuous suggestion. She was little more than a child herself. He was aware too, in passing, of the season, and the notion took hold of him that somehow the mood of the city, in its swagger of Christmas fare, had percolated through the unpleasant welter of drizzle, smoke and noise, to this high enclosure and had impressed itself on her senses, stirring there the itch for a child. He closed the curtain and fumed to face her.

"Why do you want a child?" he asked.

She shrugged and bent her head.

"For company," her eyes swung across to the display of golden animals on the floor.

"Yes, that's all you need now in your collection, isn't it?"

She nodded.

"But it's more than that too," she protested and splayed her hand over her flat stomach.

"Well, I don't," he said. "A child would only bring confusion in here."

He mounted the ladder onto the platform bed and lay with his face to the corner but did not sleep. On the floor below him she sat, moving her cast of animals about in the pale gleam of the gas flame, and watched as broad shadows were flung against the wall and ceiling.

In the twelve day approach to Christmas carol singers cluttered on the thoroughfares and the savour of mince pies sold at outdoor stalls enriched the customary dank smell of the city. Occasionally, some of these festive singers and traders turned up in the grey outer housing zones. For those in the vulgar flats the voices of the carol singers lost all coherence, the notes and words of their songs distorted by the scarfing currents of air trapped between the tall concrete blocks.

He observed a growing vagueness in her eyes and began on another evening to defend himself. "I had children once," he said. "As you might have guessed, from a marriage of twenty years. They have their moments I grant you, a trick of the voice or a look that can win your heart. But they can torment your nerves too, and when they find the weak spot they persist until you no longer know what it is you are saying or doing. You are all the children I need now."

"But me," was all that she said, and rubbed a dear space in the condensation on the glass as she tried to recompose in her head the dissonant notes that rose at intervals from the huddle of young carol singers in the darkness below.

"It would have been nice to have thrown some money to them," she remarked when the singers had moved away.

"Yes, and falling from this height the coins would probably have killed them."

She withdrew from the window and let the curtain resettle, flush with its pair.

He rarely moved now from the bed. Once in the door he undressed and climbed onto the platform. The illness that had swamped his lungs was becoming chronic. When he breathed he felt a wound stretch inside and suppurate, striking up a rattle in his chest. His skin had dried and drawn in to meet his bones. From where he lay he instructed her with monarchical detachment in the preparation of their supper but her disinterest angered him and he redoubled the rate of his smoking. As each carton was emptied he would toss it down to her, and, straightaway, her fingers would begin to manipulate the slim gold paper. His eyes then would be held by her deft movements and his attitude would once more soften towards her.

Despite his illness, he continued to work, shrugging his weakened frame into the grey coat. It did not snow in the city but a hard frost bound the roofs and roads and pavements like sheets of iron. Even in those last days before Christmas he forced himself out and back at the same hour, morning and evening, resolved not to admit of any change, for reasons of health or merrymaking, in the daily course he had established. Only by conducting each day in the same way could he uphold the pretence that time did not pass.

It was on Christmas Eve that she left him. What few material trappings she possessed were tied into a length of the red curtain and the bizarre hoard of gold foil animals was neatly pocketed in gaps and folds of the cloth. The screens alone were left behind, placed in a square like a lidless box in the centre of the eating table, where a low bolt of sunlight struck through the exposed window making their colours appear almost transparent.

When she stepped onto the pavement she shivered as much from fear as from the first sting of the winter air. She moved towards the city, skirting the main routes in case, by hazard , he would choose to surprise her and return early on this one day. Being without money she was forced to walk and the drag of the red bundle on her shoulders retarded her pace so that dusk had fallen by the time she had reached the heart of the city. In a square that she recognised she halted to sit on a step and rub her feet, swollen now with the unaccustomed exercise, and bruised with the cold. From the top of the bundle, which she had placed on the ground beside her, gleamed a fragment of gold. She smiled, and, standing again, caught the glance of a child's face through an upper floor window, As she bent to pick up her bundle she extracted the delicate beast and placed it where she had been sitting.

Frost continued to fall that night in greater profusion than it had before, and a greenish vapour pervaded every quarter of the city, merging with the scant light that showed through shutters and hallways. No traffic broke the quiet but, lining the streets, on doorsteps and on windowsills, stood a myriad of minute golden creatures, each one astir with the playful flicker of new life.

The Christmas Cuckoo

FRANCES BROWNE

ONCE UPON A TIME THERE stood in the midst of a bleak moor, in the north country, a certain village; all its inhabitants were poor, for their fields were barren, and they had little trade, but the poorest of them all were two brothers called Scrub and Spare, who followed the cobbler's craft, and had but one stall between them. It was a hut built of clay and wattles. The door was low and always open, for there was no window. The roof did not entirely keep out the rain, and the only thing comfortable about it was a wide hearth, for which the brothers could never find wood enough to make a sufficient fire. There they worked in most brotherly friendship, though with little encouragement.

The people of that village were not extravagant in shoes, and better cobblers than Scrub and Spare might be found. Spiteful people said there were no shoes so bad that they would not be worse for their mending. Nevertheless Scrub and Spare managed to live between their own trade, a small barley field, and a cottage garden, till one unlucky day when a new cobbler arrived in the village. He had lived in the capital city of the kingdom, and, by his own account, cobbled for the queen and the princesses. His awls were sharp, his lasts were new; he set up his stall in a neat cottage with two windows. The villagers soon found out that one patch of his would wear two of the brothers'. In short, all the mending left Scrub and Spare, and went to the new cobbler. The season had been wet and cold, their barley did not ripen well, and the cabbages never half closed in the garden. So the brothers were poor that winter, and when Christmas came they had nothing to feast on but a barley loaf, a piece of rusty bacon, and some small beer of their own brewing. Worse than that, the snow was very deep, and they could get no firewood. Their hut stood at the end of the village; beyond it spread the bleak moor, now all white and silent; but that moor had once been a forest. Great roots of old trees were still to be found in it, loosened from the soil and laid bare by the winds and rains—one of these, a rough, gnarled log, lay hard by their door, the half of it above the snow, and Spare said to his brother:

"Shall we sit here cold on Christmas while the great root lies yonder? Let us chop it up for firewood, the work will make us warm."

"No," said Scrub, "it's not right to chop wood on Christmas; besides, that root is too hard to be broken with any hatchet."

"Hard or not we must have a fire," replied Spare. "Come, brother, help me in with it. Poor as we are, there is nobody in the village will have such a Yule log as ours."

Scrub liked a little grandeur, and in hopes of having a fine Yule log, both brothers strained and strove with all their might till, between pulling and pushing, the great old root was safe on the hearth, and beginning to crackle and blaze with the red embers. In high glee, the cobblers sat down to their beer and bacon. The door was shut, for there was nothing but cold moonlight and snow outside; but the hut, strewn with fir boughs, and ornamented with holly, looked cheerful as the ruddy blaze flared up and rejoiced their hearts.

"Long life and good fortune to ourselves, brother!" said Spare. "I hope you will drink that toast, and may we never have a worse fire on Christmas—but what is that?"

Spare set down the drinking horn, and the brothers listened astonished, for out of the blazing root they heard, "Cuckoo! Cuckoo!" as plain as ever the spring bird's voice came over the moor on a May morning.

"It is something bad," said Scrub, terribly frightened.

"Maybe not," said Spare; and out of the deep hole at the side which the fire had not reached flew a large grey cuckoo, and lit on the table before them. Much as the cobblers had been surprised, they were still more so when it said—

"Good gentlemen, what season is this?"

"It's Christmas," said Spare.

"Then a merry Christmas to you!" said the cuckoo. "I went to sleep in the hollow of that old root one evening last summer, and never woke till the heat of your fire made me think it was summer again; but now since you have burned my lodging, let me stay in your hut till the spring comes round—I only want a hole to sleep in, and when I go on my travels next summer be assured I will bring you some present for your trouble."

"Stay, and welcome," said Spare, while Scrub sat wondering if it were something bad or not. "I'll make you a good warm hole in the thatch. But you must be hungry after that long sleep? Here is a slice of barley bread. Come help us to keep Christmas!"

The cuckoo ate up the slice, drank water from the brown jug, for he would take no beer, and flew into a snug hole which Spare scooped for him in the thatch of the hut.

Scrub said he was afraid it wouldn't be lucky; but as it slept on, and the days passed, he forgot his fears. So the snow melted, the heavy rains came, the cold grew less, the days lengthened, and one sunny morning the brothers were awoke by the cuckoo shouting its own cry to let them know the spring had come.

"Now I'm going on my travels," said the bird, "over the world to tell men of the spring. There is no country where trees bud or flowers bloom, that I will not cry in before the year goes round. Give me another slice of barley bread to keep me on my journey, and tell me what present I shall bring you at the twelvemonth's end."

Scrub would have been angry with his brother for cutting so large a slice, their store of barley meal being low, but his mind was occupied with what present would be most prudent to ask: at length, a lucky thought struck him.

"Good master cuckoo," said he, "if a great traveller who sees all the world like you, could know of any place where diamonds or pearls were to be found, one of a tolerable size brought in your beak would help such poor men as my brother and I to provide something better than barley bread for your next entertainment."

"I know nothing of diamonds or pearls," said the cuckoo, "they are in the hearts of rocks and the sands of rivers. My knowledge is only of that which grows on the earth. But there are two trees hard by the well that lies at the world's end—one of them is called the golden tree, for its leaves are all of beaten gold: every winter they fall into the well with a sound like scattered coin, and I know not what becomes of them. As for the other, it is always green like a laurel. Some call it the wise, and some the merry tree. Its leaves never fall, but they that get one of them keep a blithe heart in spite of all misfortunes, and can make themselves as merry in a hut as in a palace."

"Good master cuckoo, bring me a leaf off that tree!" cried Spare.

"Now, brother, don't be a fool!" said Scrub. "Think of the leaves of beaten gold! Dear master cuckoo, bring me one of them!"

Before another word could be spoken, the cuckoo had flown out of the open door, and was shouting its spring cry over moor and meadow. The brothers were poorer than ever that year; nobody would send them a single shoe to mend. The new cobbler said, in scorn, they should come to be his apprentices; and Scrub and Spare would have left the village but for their barley field, their cabbage garden, and a certain maid called Fairfeather, whom both the cobblers had courted for seven years without even knowing which she meant to favour.

Sometimes Fairfeather seemed inclined to Scrub, sometimes she smiled on Spare; but the brothers never disputed for that. They sowed their barley, planted their cabbage, and now that their trade was gone, worked in the rich villagers' fields to make out a scanty living. So the seasons came and passed: spring, summer, harvest, and winter followed one another as they have done from the beginning. At the end of the latter, Scrub and Spare had grown so poor and ragged that Fairfeather thought them beneath her notice. Old neighbours forgot to invite them to wedding feasts or merrymaking; and they thought the cuckoo had forgotten them, too, when at daybreak, on the first of April, they heard a hard beak knocking at their door, and a voice crying:

"Cuckoo! Cuckoo! Let me in with my presents."

Spare ran to open the door, and in came the cuckoo, carrying on one side of his bill a golden leaf larger than that of any tree in the north country; and in the other, one like that of the common laurel, only it had a fresher green.

"Here," it said, giving the gold to Scrub and the green to Spare, "it is a long carriage from the world's end. Give me a slice of barley bread, for I must tell the north country that the spring has come."

Scrub did not grudge the thickness of that slice, though it was cut from their last loaf. So much gold had never been in the cobbler's hands before, and he could not help exulting over his brother.

"See the wisdom of my choice!" he said, holding up the large leaf of gold. "As for yours, as good might be plucked from any hedge. I wonder a sensible bird would carry the like so far."

"Good master cobbler," cried the cuckoo, finishing the slice, "your conclusions are more hasty than courteous. If your brother be disappointed this time, I go on the same journey every year, and for your hospitable entertainment will think it no trouble to bring each of you whichever leaf you desire."

"Darling cuckoo!" cried Scrub, "bring me a golden one"; and Spare, looking up from the green leaf on which he gazed as though it were a crown jewel, said:

"Be sure to bring me one from the merry tree," and away flew the cuckoo.

"This is the Feast of All Fools, and it ought to be your birthday," said Scrub. "Did ever man fling away such an opportunity of getting rich! Much good your merry leaves will do in the midst of rags and poverty!" So he went on, but Spare laughed at him, and answered with quaint old proverbs concerning the cares that come with gold, till Scrub, at length getting angry, vowed his brother was not fit to live with a respectable man; and taking his lasts, his awls, and his golden leaf, he left the wattle hut, and went to tell the villagers.

They were astonished at the folly of Spare and charmed with Scrub's good sense, particularly when he showed them the golden leaf, and told that the cuckoo would bring him one every spring. The new cobbler immediately took him into partnership; the greatest people sent him their shoes to mend; Fairfeather smiled graciously upon him, and in the course of that summer they were married, with a grand wedding feast, at which the whole village danced, except Spare, who was not invited, because the bride could not bear his low-mindedness, and his brother thought him a disgrace to the family.

Indeed, all who heard the story concluded that Spare must be mad, and nobody would associate with him but a lame tinker, a beggar boy, and a poor woman reputed to be a witch because she was old and ugly. As for Scrub, he established himself with Fairfeather in a cottage close by that of the new cobbler, and quite as fine. There he mended shoes to everybody's satisfaction, had a scarlet coat for holidays, and a fat goose for dinner every wedding day. Fairfeather, too, had a crimson gown and fine blue ribands; but neither she nor Scrub were content, for to buy this grandeur the golden leaf had to be broken and parted with piece by piece, so the last morsel was gone before the cuckoo came with another.

Spare lived on in the old hut, and worked in the cabbage garden. (Scrub had got the barley field because he was the eldest.) Every day his coat grew more ragged, and the hut more weather-beaten; but people remarked that he never looked sad or sour; and the wonder was, that from the time they began to keep his company, the tinker grew kinder to the poor ass with which he travelled the country, the beggar boy kept out of mischief, and the old woman was never cross to her cat or angry with the children.

Every first of April the cuckoo came tapping at their doors with the golden leaf to Scrub and the green to Spare. Fairfeather would have entertained him nobly with wheaten bread and honey, for she had some notion of persuading him to bring two gold leaves instead of one; but the cuckoo flew away to eat barley bread with Spare, saying he was not fit company for fine people, and liked the old hut where he slept so snugly from Christmas till Spring.

Scrub spent the golden leaves, and Spare kept the merry ones; and I know not how many years passed in this manner, when a certain great lord, who owned that village came to the neighbourhood. His castle stood on the moor. It was ancient and strong, with high towers and a deep moat. All the country, as far as one could see from the highest turret, belonged to its lord; but he had not been there for twenty years, and would not have come then, only he was melancholy. The cause of his grief was that he had been prime minister at court, and in high favour, till somebody told the crown prince that he had spoken disrespectfully concerning the turning out of his royal highness's toes, and the king that he did not lay on taxes enough, whereon the north country lord was turned out of office, and banished to his own estate. There he lived for some weeks in very bad temper. The servants said nothing would please him, and the villagers put on their worst clothes lest he should raise their rents; but one day in the harvest time his lordship chanced to meet Spare gathering watercresses at a meadow stream, and fell into talk with the cobbler.

How it was nobody could tell, but from the hour of that discourse the great lord cast away his melancholy: he forgot his lost office and his court enemies, the king's taxes and the crown prince's toes, and went about with a noble train hunting, fishing, and making merry in his hall, where all travellers were entertained and all the poor were welcome. This strange story spread through the north country, and great company came to the cobbler's hut—rich men who had lost their money, poor men who had lost their friends, beauties who had grown old, wits who had gone out of fashion, all came to talk with Spare, and whatever their troubles had been, all went home merry. The rich gave him presents, the poor gave him thanks. Spare's coat ceased to be ragged, he had bacon with his cabbage, and the villagers began to think there was some sense in him.

By this time his fame had reached the capital city, and even the court. There were a great many discontented people there besides the king, who had lately fallen into ill-humour because a neighbouring princess, with seven islands for her dowry, would not marry his eldest son. So a royal messenger was sent to Spare, with a velvet mantle, a diamond ring, and a command that he should repair to court immediately.

"Tomorrow is the first of April," said Spare, "and I will go with you two hours after sunrise."

The messenger lodged all night at the castle, and the cuckoo came at sunrise with the merry leaf.

"Court is a fine place," he said when the cobbler told him he was going, "but I cannot come there, they would lay snares and catch me; So be careful of the leaves I have brought you, and give me a farewell slice of barley bread."

Spare was sorry to part with the cuckoo, little as he had of his company, but he gave him a slice which would have broken Scrub's heart in former times, it was so thick and large; and having sewed up the leaves in the lining of his leather doublet, he set out with the messenger on his way to court.

His coming caused great surprise there. Everybody wondered what the king could see in such a common-looking man; but scarce had his majesty conversed with him half an hour, when the princess and her seven islands were forgotten, and orders given that a feast for all comers should be spread in the banquet hall. The princes of the blood, the great lords and ladies, ministers of state, and judges of the land, after that discoursed with Spare, and the more they talked the lighter grew their hearts, so that such changes had never been seen at court. The lords forgot their spites and the ladies their envies, the princes and ministers made friends among themselves, and the judges showed no favour.

As for Spare, he had a chamber assigned him in the palace, and a seat at the king's table; one sent him rich robes and another costly jewels; but in the midst of all his grandeur he still wore the leathern doublet, which the palace servants thought remarkably mean. One day the king's attention being drawn to it by the chief page, his majesty inquired why Spare didn't give it to a beggar? But the cobbler answered:

"High and mighty monarch, this doublet was with me before silk and velvet came—I find it easier to wear than the court cut; moreover, it serves to keep me humble, by recalling the days when it was my holiday garment."

The king thought this a wise speech, and commanded that no one should find fault with the leathern doublet. So things went, till tidings of his brother's good fortune reached Scrub in the moorland cottage on another first of April, when the cuckoo came with two golden leaves, because he had none to carry for Spare.

"Think of that!" said Fairfeather. "Here we are spending our lives in this humdrum place, and Spare making his fortune at court with two or three paltry green leaves! What would they say to our golden ones? Let us pack up and make our way to the king's palace; I'm sure he will make you a lord and me a lady of honour, not to speak of all the fine clothes and presents we shall have."

Scrub thought this excellent reasoning, and their packing up began: but it was soon found that the cottage contained few things fit for carrying to court. Fairfeather could not think of her wooden bowls, spoons, and trenchers being seen there. Scrub considered his lasts and awls better left behind, as without them, he concluded, no one would suspect him of being a cobbler. So putting on their holiday clothes, Fairfeather took her looking glass and Scrub his drinking horn, which happened to have a very thin rim of silver, and each carrying a golden leaf carefully wrapped up that none might see it till they reached the palace, the pair set out in great expectation.

How far Scrub and Fairfeather journeyed I cannot say, but when the sun was high and warm at noon, they came into a wood both tired and hungry.

"If I had known it was so far to court," said Scrub, "I would have brought the end of that barley loaf which we left in the cupboard."

"Husband," said Fairfeather, "you shouldn't have such mean thoughts: How could one eat barley bread on the way to a palace? Let us rest ourselves under this tree, and look at our golden leaves to see if they are safe." In looking at the leaves, and talking of their fine prospects, Scrub and Fairfeather did not perceive that a very thin old woman had slipped from behind the tree, with a long staff in her hand and a great wallet by her side.

"Noble lord and lady," she said, "for I know ye are such by your voices, though my eyes are dim and my hearing none of the sharpest, will ye condescend to tell me where I may find some water to mix a bottle of mead which I carry in my wallet, because it is too strong for me?"

As the old woman spoke, she pulled out a large wooden bottle such as shepherds used in the ancient times, corked with leaves rolled together, and having a small wooden cup hanging from its handle.

"Perhaps ye will do me the favour to taste," she said. "It is only made of the best honey. I have also cream cheese, and a wheaten loaf here, if such honourable persons as you would eat the like."

Scrub and Fairfeather became very condescending after this speech. They were now sure that there must be some appearance of nobility about them; besides, they were very hungry, and having hastily wrapped up the golden leaves, they assured the old woman they were not at all proud, notwithstanding the lands and castles they had left behind them in the north country, and would willingly help to lighten the wallet. The old woman could scarcely be persuaded to sit down for pure humility, but at length she did, and before the wallet was half empty, Scrub and Fairfeather firmly believed that there must be something remarkably noble-looking about them. This was not entirely owing to her ingenious discourse. The old woman was a wood-witch; her name was Buttertongue, and all her time was spent in making mead, which, being boiled with curious herbs and spells, had the power of making all who drank it fall asleep and dream with their eyes open. She had two dwarfs of sons; one was named Spy, and the other Pounce. Wherever their mother went they were not far behind; and whoever tasted her mead was sure to be robbed by the dwarfs.

Scrub and Fairfeather sat leaning against the old tree. The cobbler had a lump of cheese in his hand; his wife held fast a hunch of bread. Their eyes and mouths were both open, but they were dreaming of great grandeur at court, when the old woman raised her shrill voice:

"What ho, my sons! Come here and carry home the harvest."

No sooner had she spoken, than the two little dwarfs darted out of the neighbouring thicket.

"Idle boys!" cried the mother, "what have ye done today to help our living?"

"I have been to the city," said Spy, "and could see nothing. These are hard times for us—everybody minds their business so contentedly since that cobbler came; but here is a leathern doublet which his page threw out of the window; it's of no use, but I brought it to let you see I was not idle." And he tossed down Spare's doublet, with the merry leaves in it, which he had carried like a bundle on his little back.

To explain how Spy came by it, I must tell you that the forest was not far from the great city where Spare lived in such high esteem. All things had gone well with the cobbler till the king thought that it was quite unbecoming to see such a worthy man without a servant. His majesty, therefore, to let all men understand his royal favour toward Spare, appointed one of his own pages to wait upon him. The name of this youth was Tinseltoes, and, though he was the seventh of the king's pages, nobody in all the court had grander notions. Nothing could please him that had not gold or silver about it, and his grandmother feared he would hang himself for being appointed page to a cobbler. As for Spare, if anything could have troubled him, this token of his majesty's kindness would have done it.

The honest man had been so used to serve himself that the page was always in the way, but his merry leaves came to his assistance; and, to the great surprise of his grandmother, Tinseltoes took wonderfully to the new service. Some said it was because Spare gave him nothing to do but play at bowls all day on the palace green. Yet one thing grieved the heart of Tinseltoes, and that was his master's leathern doublet, but for it he was persuaded people would never remember that Spare had been a cobbler, and the page took a deal of pains to let him see how unfashionable it was at court; but Spare answered Tinseltoes as he had done the king, and at last, finding nothing better would do, the page got up one fine morning earlier than his master, and tossed the leathern doublet out of the back window into a certain lane where Spy found it, and brought it to his mother.

"That nasty thing!" said the old woman. "Where is the good in it?"

By this time, Pounce had taken everything of value from Scrub and Fairfeather—the looking glass, the silver-rimmed horn, the husband's scarlet coat, the wife's gay mantle, and, above all, the golden leaves, which so rejoiced old Buttertongue and her sons, that they threw the leathern doublet over the sleeping cobbler for a jest, and went off to their hut in the heart of the forest.

The sun was going down when Scrub and Fairfeather awoke from dreaming that they had been made a lord and a lady, and sat clothed in silk and velvet, feasting with the king in his palace hall. It was a great disappointment to find their golden leaves and all their best things gone. Scrub tore his hair, and vowed to take the old woman's life, while Fairfeather lamented sore; but Scrub, feeling cold for want of his coat, put on the leathern doublet without asking or caring whence it came.

Scarcely was it buttoned on when a change came over him; he addressed such merry discourse to Fairfeather, that, instead of lamentations, she made the wood ring with laughter. Both busied themselves in getting up a hut of boughs, in which Scrub kindled a fire with a flint and steel, which, together with his pipe, he had brought unknown to Fairfeather, who had told him the like was never heard of at court. Then they found a pheasant's nest at the root of an old oak, made a meal of roasted eggs, and went to sleep on a heap of long green grass which they had gathered, with nightingales singing all night long in the old trees about them. So it happened that Scrub and Fairfeather stayed day after day in the forest, making their hut larger and more comfortable against the winter, living on wild birds' eggs and berries, and never thinking of their lost golden leaves, or their journey to court.

In the meantime Spare had got up and missed his doublet. Tinseltoes, of course, said he knew nothing about it. The whole palace was searched, and every servant questioned, till all the court wondered why such a fuss was made about an old leathern doublet. That very day things came back to their old fashion. Quarrels began among the lords, and jealousies among the ladies. The king said his subjects did not pay him half enough taxes, the queen wanted more jewels, the servants took to their old bickerings and got up some new ones. Spare found himself getting wonderfully dull, and very much out of place: nobles began to ask what business a cobbler had at the king's table, and his majesty ordered the palace chronicles to be searched for a precedent. The cobbler was too wise to tell all he had lost with that doublet, but being by this time somewhat familiar with court customs, he proclaimed a reward of fifty gold pieces to any who would bring him news concerning it.

Scarcely was this made known in the city, when the gates and outer courts of the palace were filled by men, women, and children, some bringing leathern doublets of every cut and colour; some with tales of what they had heard and seen in their walks about the neighbourhood; and so much news concerning all sorts of great people came out of these stories, that lords and ladies ran to the king with complaints of Spare as a speaker of slander; and his majesty, being now satisfied that there was no example in all the palace records of such a retainer, issued a decree banishing the cobbler forever from court, and confiscating all his goods in favour of Tinseltoes.

That royal edict was scarcely published before the page was in full possession of his rich chamber, his costly garments, and all the presents the courtiers had given him; while Spare, having no longer the fifty pieces of gold to give, was glad to make his escape out of the back window, for fear of the nobles, who vowed to be revenged on him, and the crowd, who were prepared to stone him for cheating them about his doublet.

The window from which Spare let himself down with a strong rope, was that from which Tinseltoes had tossed the doublet, and as the cobbler came down late in the twilight, a poor woodman, with a heavy load of fagots, stopped and stared at him in great astonishment.

"What's the matter, friend?" said Spare. "Did you never see a man coming down from a back window before?"

"Why," said the woodman, "the last morning I passed here a leathern doublet came out of that very window, and I'll be bound you are the owner of it."

"That I am, friend," said the cobbler. "Can you tell me which way that doublet went?"

"As I walked on," said the woodman, "a dwarf, called Spy, bundled it up and ran off to his mother in the forest."

"Honest friend," said Spare, taking off the last of his fine clothes (a grass-green mantle edged with gold), "I'll give you this if you will follow the dwarf, and bring me back my doublet."

"It would not be good to carry fagots in," said the woodman. "But if you want back your doublet, the road to the forest lies at the end of this lane," and he trudged away.

Determined to find his doublet, and sure that neither crowd nor courtiers could catch him in the forest, Spare went on his way, and was soon among the tall trees; but neither hut nor dwarf could he see. Moreover, the night came on; the wood was dark and tangled, but here and there the moon shone through its alleys, the great owls flitted about, and the nightingales sang. So he went on, hoping to find some place of shelter. At last the red light of a fire, gleaming through a thicket, led him to the door of a low hut. It stood half open, as if there was nothing to fear, and within he saw his brother Scrub snoring loudly on a bed of grass, at the foot of which lay his own leathern doublet; while Fairfeather, in a kirtle made of plaited rushes, sat roasting pheasants' eggs by the fire.

"Good evening, mistress," said Spare, stepping in.

The blaze shone on him, but so changed was her brother-in-law with his court life, that Fairfeather did not know him, and she answered far more courteously than was her wont.

"Good evening, master. Whence come ye so late? But speak low, for my good man has sorely tired himself cleaving wood, and is taking a sleep, as you see, before supper."

"A good rest to him," said Spare, perceiving he was not known. "I come from the court for a day's hunting, and have lost my way in the forest."

"Sit down and have a share of our supper," said Fairfeather. "I will put some more eggs in the ashes; and tell me the news of court—I used to think of it long ago when I was young and foolish."

"Did you never go there?" said the cobbler. "So fair a dame as you would make the ladies marvel."

"You are pleased to flatter," said Fairfeather, "but my husband has a brother there, and we left our moorland village to try our fortune also. An old woman enticed us with fair words and strong drink at the entrance of this forest, where we fell asleep and dreamt of great things; but when we woke, everything had been robbed from us: my looking glass, my scarlet cloak, my husband's Sunday coat; and, in place of all, the robbers left him that old leathern doublet, which he has worn ever since, and never was so merry in all his life, though we live in this poor hut."

"It is a shabby doublet, that," said Spare, taking up the garment, and seeing that it was his own, for the merry leaves were still sewed in its lining. "It would be good for hunting in, however—your husband would be glad to part with it, I dare say, in exchange for this handsome cloak," and he pulled off the green mantle and buttoned on the doublet, much to Fairfeather"s delight, who ran and shook Scrub, crying:

"Husband! Husband! Rise and see what a good bargain I have made."

Scrub gave one closing snore, and muttered something about the root being hard; but he rubbed his eyes, gazed up at his brother, and said:

"Spare, is that really you? How did you like the court, and have you made your fortune?"

"That I have, brother," said Spare, "in getting back my own good leathern doublet. Come, let us eat eggs, and rest ourselves here this night. In the morning we will return to our own old hut, at the end of the moorland village where the Christmas Cuckoo will come and bring us leaves."

Scrub and Fairfeather agreed. So in the morning they all returned, and found the old hut little the worse for wear and weather. The neighbours came about them to ask the news of court, and see if they had made their fortune. Everybody was astonished to find the three poorer than ever, but somehow they liked to go back to the hut. Spare brought out the lasts and awls he had hidden in a corner; Scrub and he began their old trade, and the whole north country found out that there never were such cobblers.

They mended the shoes of lords and ladies as well as the common people; everybody was satisfied. Their custom increased from day to day, and all that were disappointed, discontented, or unlucky, came to the hut as in old times, before Spare went to court.

The rich brought them presents; the poor did them service. The hut itself changed, no one knew how. Flowering honeysuckle grew over its roof; red and white roses grew thick about its door. Moreover, the Christmas Cuckoo always came on the first of April, bringing three leaves of the merry tree—for Scrub and Fairfeather would have no more golden ones. So it was with them when I last heard the news of the north country.

Christmas Pudding

COLM TÓIBÍN

CHRISTMAS MEANT THAT THE WHOLE family was together—my parents and their five children, and also my father's brother and sister and my mother's sister. On Christmas Day in Enniscorthy, at one o'clock—the same time as every other Irish family—we ate the same food: turkey and ham and vegetables, including mashed and roast potatoes. The only difference between us and everybody else was that our Christmas pudding was better. My grandmother had known the cook at the Castle, and the cook had slipped her the recipe for the plum pudding that the Roches ate each year.

The Castle in Enniscorthy, in its current form, was built by the Wallop family, later the Earls of Portsmouth, in the late sixteenth century, and was, for a few hundred years, the center of English rule in our part of the valley. It squatted at the top of Castle Hill, right in the middle of town, with its two staircases, its many grand rooms, and a dungeon. In the early twentieth century, it was restored and expanded by the Roche family, who lived there for almost fifty years. The Roches were a byword for wealth in Enniscorthy. If I ever wanted something new or expensive, my mother would say, "Who do you think we are? The Roches of the Castle?" And I would know then that the item in question was not coming my way. Thus, the idea that we were eating the same pudding on Christmas Day as the Roches was a matter of some pride.

The recipe, it seemed, had come from America, and it included the usual quantity of nuts and raisins, currants and candied fruit. But whereas the normal Irish recipe called for suet, ours used butter, which was much more expensive. The pudding was boiled for hours, a few weeks before Christmas, and then reheated. Served with cream or brandy butter or flamed with burning brandy, it was pure, unmitigated luxury—soft, moist, almost soggy with goodness. Christmas pudding with suet could be dark in color and somewhat bitter, even greasy; with butter, it was sweetly textured, some of it melting on your tongue while the rest—the nuts and raisins and candied fruit—remained firm and chewy. Even now, thinking about it, I want some.

The only thing to interfere with the sense of well-being and togetherness induced by this pudding came from my father's side of the family. My father and his siblings thought that rude words were funny. My mother and her sister believed they were vulgar. Therefore, all rude words, even the smallest and humblest of them, were banned in our house. I suppose it was the wine that gave my father and his siblings courage each year on Christmas Day. In their family, they'd had a tradition of saying the same thing each time the Christmas pudding appeared. It seemed that they'd had a neighbor called Val, who was a notorious crank. Even on Christmas Day, nothing pleased him. Every year, after a long and sumptuous dinner, his wife produced the Christmas pudding and called on him to divide it into sections. She'd say, "Cut the pudding, Val," and he'd invariably reply, "Cut my shite!" My father and his siblings thought this response gloriously funny.

Sometimes, as Christmas approached, my mother would ask my father if, for once, we could be spared the repetition of this exchange, so unnecessary and such a bad example to the children. My father would promise to do what he could. But on Christmas Day, when my mother was back in the kitchen, the main course completed, the dishes of turkey and ham cleared from the table, and the smell of the Roches' plum pudding wafting in, a glint would appear in his eye. His sister would already be laughing quietly, and we five children would wait with glee. Then the pudding would appear, the tension rising as my mother removed the covering and began to divide it among the ten of us. It's hard to know what I loved more: the pudding itself, the word that would accompany it, or the howls of laughter, met with bitter silence, that would ensue. I think I liked the word best.

"Cut the pudding, Val," my father's brother would say, and then my father and his brother and sister would all call out in unison, "Cut my shite!" They'd roar with laughter, tears running down their cheeks. My mother would take her revenge by announcing that she had bought herself a very good book for Christmas and she was going to spend the rest of the day reading it, and we could all do as we pleased but she would not be setting foot in the kitchen again. "It's the maid's day off," she'd say sourly. In the meantime, when the glee had subsided, the plum pudding from the Roches of the Castle was delicious.

The Magi

W. B. YEATS

Now as at all times I can see in the mind's eye,
In their stiff, painted clothes, the pale unsatisfied ones
Appear and disappear in the blue depths of the sky
With all their ancient faces like rain-beaten stones,
And all their helms of silver hovering side by side,
And all their eyes still fixed, hoping to find once more,
Being by Calvary's turbulence unsatisfied,
The uncontrollable mystery on the bestial floor.

Candle and Crib

K. F. PURDON

Chapter I

MOLONEY'S

IT WOULD BE HARD TO find a pleasanter, more friendly-looking place in all Ardenoo than Moloney's of the Crooked Boreen, where Big Michael and the wife lived, a piece up from the high road. And well might you call the little causey "crooked" that led to their door, for rough and stony that boreen was, twisting and winding along by the bog-side, this way and that way, the same as if it couldn't rightly make up its mind where it wanted to bring you. So it was all the more of a surprise when you did get to Moloney's, to find a house with such an appearance of comfort upon it, in such a place.

Long and low that house was, and very old. You could tell the great age of it by the thickness of the thatch, as well as by seeing, when you were standing inside upon the kitchen floor and looking up, that that same thatch was resting, not upon common planks, sawn with the grain and against the grain and every way, but upon the real boughs themselves, put there by them that had to choose carefully what would be suitable for their purpose, because there were few tools then for shaping timber. So that's how the branches were there yet, the same as ever, bark and twigs and all; ay, and as sound as the day they were put there, two hundred years before.

As for the walls at Moloney's ... mud, I'm not denying it! But the thickness of them! And the way they were kept whitewashed, inside and out! They'd dazzle you, to look at them: especially in the kitchen of an evening, when the fire would be strong. And that was a thing that occurred mostly always at Moloney's. For Herself was a most notorious Vanithee; and there's no better sign of good housekeeping than a clean, blazing hearth. Sure isn't that, as a body might say, the heart of the whole house? Heart or hearth, isn't it all the one thing, nearly? For if warmth and comfort for the body come from the one, doesn't love and pleasant kindness come from the other? Ay, indeed!

And now here was the Christmas Eve come round again, when everyone puts the best foot foremost, whether they can or not. And so by Moloney's. The darkness had fallen, and a wild, wet night it was, as ever came out of the heavens. But that only made the light seem the brighter and more coaxing that the fire was sending out over the half door, and through the little, twinkling bulls'-eyes windows, as if it was trying to say, "Come along in, whoever you are that's outside in the cold and the rain! Look at the way the Woman has the floor swept, till there isn't a speck upon it! And the tables and stools scoured like the snow, and the big old pewter plates and dishes upon the dresser polished till they're shining like a goat's eyes from under a bed! Come in! Sure everyone is welcome here tonight, whether they come or not!"

And still in all...!

Well, one look round would tell you, with half an eye, that something was wrong at Moloney's, Christmas Eve and all as it was. For Big Michael himself was standing there in the kitchen, cracking his red, wet fingers one after the other, and looking most uncomfortable. The wet was running down from his big frieze coat, but it wasn't that he minded. He was too well used to soft weather to care about wet clothes. Beside him upon the floor was the big market-basket, with all manner of paper parcels, blue and brown, sticking out from under the lid that wouldn't shut down, he had brought home so much from Melia's shop. But that basket had a forgotten look about it, because there beside it stood Herself, and she not asking to unpack it or do a thing with it.

She was a little bit of a woman, that you'd think you could blow off the palm of your hand with one puff of your breath. As thin as a whip she was, and as straight as a rush; and she was looking up now at Michael with flaming cheeks and eyes like troubled waters.

"No letter!" she was saying. "And is it that you brought home no letter, after you being to the post! Sure it can't be but they wrote to say were they coming or not, after they being asked here for the Christmas! Sure I thought you'd surely have word to say when to expect them; and was thinking even that they might be coming with yourself! Only I suppose the little ass and dray wouldn't be grand enough for the wife! Of coorse I didn't think of *her* writing; she may know no better, and isn't to be blemt if she has no manners; she can't help the way she was brought up! But Art! Sure there must be a letter from him…!"

"Wait and I'll try again!" said Big Michael slowly; and then he took to feel through his pockets again for the letter their son was to have sent them. But when he had done this, he could only shake his head, so that the rain-drops fell from his hair and beard—turning brackety grey, they were, Michael being on in years.

"No, in trath! Not as much as one letter have I this night!" he said slowly.

At this the Woman began to laugh, in spite of the great annoyance that was on her.

"Sure," she said, "if Mrs. Melia had a letter for us, wouldn't she have given it to you? What use would *she* have for it? And if she hadn't, and told you so, where's the sense in you feeling your pockets over and over? A body'd think you expected letters to grow there, the same as American apples in barrels! How could you have there what you didn't put there? But let you go on off ou'er this now! Look at the state you have the clean floor in, with the rain dreeping from your *cota-mor*!"

"Coming down it is, like as if it was out of a sieve!" said Michael. "And wasn't it God that done it, that I took the notion to cut the holly'n'ivy while the day was someways fine, afore I started off to the shop! Has it safe below … so I'll just go for it now, the way we can be settling out the Crib and all …"

"There'll no holly'n'ivy go up on these walls tonight, if I'm to be let have a say in the business!" said Mrs. Moloney. "Sich trash and nonsense! Making mess and trouble for them that has plenty to do without that! And as for the Crib, let it stop where it is …"

On the word she went back to her stool in the chimney corner, where she always sat bolt upright, and took up her knitting, the same as if it wasn't the Christmas Eve at all. For Art, their only child, that stocking was meant. But her hands were shaking so much that she dropped more stitches off the needles than she made, and still she persevered. Big Michael looked at her for a bit, very pitiful; even opened his mouth once, as if he wanted to say something; a nice, silent person he was, very even-going in himself. But he must have thought better of it, for he only shook his head again, and turned and went off out of the door into the wild storm and darkness, with the wind howling and threatening all about the bog and countryside, the shockingest ever you knew.

And as soon as he was gone, didn't the Woman throw down her knitting, and laid her head upon her knees, and cried and cried, till her blue checky apron was like as if it was after being wrung out of a tub of suds.

"Och, Art!" she'd cry. "Isn't this the queer way for you to be going on! To say you never answered the letter that was wrote to you! This very day five-and-twenty years you came here to us! As lovely as a little angel you were! The grand, big blue eyes of you! And the way you'd laugh up at me and put out the little hand…! And you the only one ever God sent us! And never a word between us, only when you took the notion to go off to Dublin; sure it near broke our hearts, but what could we do, only give you our blessing! And … and then hearing the good accounts of the way you were going on…. But it's the wife that done it all, and has him that changed…! Too grand she is, no doubt, for the likes of us! Och, grand how-are-ye! No, but not half good enough for Art! He that was always counted a choice boy by all that knew him! And any word them that saw the wife beyant in Dublin with him brought back, was no great things. A poor-looking little scollop of a thing, they tell me she is; and like as if she'd have about as much iday of taking butter off a churn, or spinning a hank of yarn, as a pig would have of a holiday! What opinion could any sensible body have of that kind of a wedding, without even a match-maker to inquire into the thing, to see was it anyways suitable or not! Och, Art! Art! It's little I thought, this day five-and-twenty years, the way the thing would be now!"

Chapter II

THE STABLE

WHILE POOR MRS. MOLONEY WAS fretting like this, and it Christmas Eve and all, Big Michael was making his way through the wind and the sleety rain to where he had his stable, a piece off from the house. It was pitch-dark, so that he couldn't see his hand before his eyes, if he held it up; but he had his lantern, and anyway he knew his way about blindfold. But even in daylight you might pass by that stable ready, unless you knew it was there. For it was very little, and being roofed with heather it looked only like a bit of the bog that had humped itself up a bit higher than the rest.

Poor-looking and small as it was, Big Michael was very proud of that stable. He and Art had built it together, just before Art leaving home. It was wanted to keep the little wad of hay or straw safe from the weather, as well as to shelter the cow of a hard night. And after Art had gone off to the Big Smoke, and for no other reason only getting restless, as young hearts often do, many and many a time Michael would slope off to the stable, and sit down there to take a draw of the pipe and to wish he had his pleasant, active young boy back at home again. He missed Art full as much as the mother, and maybe more.

In fact, it was getting into a habit with Michael to go off to the stable. He had the best of a wife, but still there were times when he'd wish to be with himself somewhere, so that he could take his ease, and still not be feeling himself an annoyance to a busy woman. Big Michael himself, the people said, always looked as if he thought tomorrow would do. But the Woman that owned him was of a different way of thinking, always going at something. So he got the fashion of keeping out of her way.

When he got to the stable this night, a bit out of breath with the great wind, he took notice first of the cow, and he saw that she was comfortable, plenty of straw to lie upon, and plenty of fodder before her. So then he bethought him of the little ass that was outside under the dray yet.

"I'll put her in, too!" he thought. "Destroyed she is and quite weakly with the wet, like all donkeys, God help them! Let alone the mud and gutter she's after travelling through, all that long ways from the shop! And carrit the things we were in need of, too! I'll let her stand here near the cow. A good dry bed I'll put under her, and give her a grain of oats to pet her heart. It'll not go astray with her, and she has it well earned, the creature!"

So he unyoked the ass and led her into the stable, and rubbed down her shaggy coat, all dripping like his own clothes, and fed her, and watched with a curious satisfaction the nice way, like a lady, that she took the feed he put before her.

"Poor Winny!" he said, rubbing a finger up and down her soft ears. "Many's the time Art laughed at you, and said it was only one remove from a wheel-barra to be driving you! Ling-gerin' Death is what he used to call you! But sure you do your best! And if you were the fastest horse ever won the Grand National, you could do no more!"

He looked round then, with a very satisfied feeling. There he had them, the two poor animals that depended out of him, but that served him and his so well, too; had them safe and warm from the storm and rain outside. He swung the lantern to and fro, so that he could see everything that was in the stable. One end of it was filled with hay and straw. The light gleamed here, gleamed there upon the kind, homely plenty he had stored. Then it fell upon a heap of something else; something that glistened from many points, green and cheerful.

"The holly'n'ivy," Big Michael thought, "that I cut this morning, and has it here, the way it would be handy to do out the place in greenery against Art and the wife would be here! Well, well! I wouldn't wish to go against Herself, and she so fretted; but sure I might as well not have cut it at all!"

He stood and stared at it, very mournful in himself. For the best part of the Christmas to Michael was not the good feeding Herself always provided, though he could take his share of that, as well as another; no, but the holly and ivy and the Candle and the Crib; and now she had set her face against them all. And it wouldn't be Christmas at all, he thought, without them!

A sudden thought came into his mind.

"Why can't I have it Christmas here," he said to himself, "and not be letting all these beautiful green branches go to waste! That's what I'll do!"

And with that, he laid down the lantern, and began to decorate the little stable. He moved slowly, but the work grew under his hands. He put the bright, glistening holly in the rack that the cow fed from, and over the door. And he flung the long curving trails of ivy over the rafters, so that they hung down, and the whole place became the most loveliest bower of green that you might ask to see.

He had just put up the last of his green stuff, when the lantern flickered up and then quenched; it was burnt out.

"Dear, dear!" thought Michael. "A pity it is to say there's no light to see it by; even if there's no one to look at it, itself!"

He stood still a bit. It always took Michael a good while even to think. Then he said to himself, "Wait a bit! go aisy, now, will ye!" as if the wife was there to be prodding him on. And then he began slowly to unbutton his coat, and then another under that, and another, and so on, much like peeling skins off an onion, till at last he came to something that he drew out very carefully; something long and slim, and that gleamed white in the light of a match he struck against the wall.

"*There's* a Christmas Candle for ye!" he said, looking admiringly at it. "Two foot long if it's an inch! Mrs. Melia does the thing right, if she goes to do it at all, the decent, nice poor woman that she is! Gave me that Candle in a Christmas present; her Christmas box she said it was, and says she, 'It'll do to welcome Art and the young wife home!' says she. And so of course it would, if only it was a thing that they were coming.... But sure, God knows what happened to stop them.... But I thought it as good say nothing about the Candle, foreninst Herself, to be making her worse, when I seen the way she was about the Crib itself! It's a pity she not to see it ..."

Slowly and awkwardly Big Michael contrived to light the Candle and to set it up in a bucket that was there handy. He steadied it there by melting some of the grease around it, and made it firm so that it could not upset to do damage to the stable. Then when it was burning well he went off, turning when he got out into the storm and darkness outside to look again at the Candle that was shedding a ray of lovely light far into the night.

"Ay, indeed!" thought he to himself, with great satisfaction, "it is a grand fine Christmas Candle, sure enough! And it would be noways right for us, even if we are only with ourselves to-night, not to have one lit, the same as every other house in Ardenoo has, the way if any poor woman with a child in her arms was wandering by, far from her own place, she'd see the light and know there was room and a welcome waiting there for them both! Ay, indeed! A great Candle that is, and will last well and shine across the whole bog! But I wish Mrs. Melia had given me the letter as well!"

Chapter III

THE LETTER

THE QUEER THING IS THAT Big Michael, slow and all as he was, happened to be right about the letter from Art. It had been written, and, moreover, it had reached Ardenoo post office. But no one knew that for certain, or what became of it, only a small little pup of a terrier dog belonging to one of the Melia boys. This pup was just of an age that it was a great comfort to his mouth to have something he could chew. He was lying taking his ease, just under the counter where the letters got sorted. And when, as luck would have it, Art's letter slipped down, of all others, from the big heap of papers and all sorts that came very plenty at that Christmas season, this little dog had no delay, only begin on the letter. In two minutes he had "little dan" made of it! Nothing left of it only a couple or three little wet rags that got swep' out the next morning, and never were heard of again. Sure, why would they, when only the pup knew anything about them? And he couldn't explain the thing, even if he had wanted to. He escaped a few kicks by that. Still, dogs often get into trouble the same way, God help them, without having earned it at all!

Yes, the invitation for the Christmas was answered. The wife, Delia her name was, had said nothing at first when it came. To tell the truth, she was well satisfied where she was, with Art and the child all to herself, in their one room in a back street. Up a lot of stairs it was, too, and the other people in the house not to say too tasty in their way of going on. But poor Delia thought it was all grand, with the little bits of furniture herself and Art would buy according as they could manage it, and the cradle in the corner by the fire.

Poor Art would smother there betimes, nigh-hand, when he'd think of the Crooked Boreen, and the wide silence of the bog, with the soft sweet wind blowing across it, and the cows and all, and the neighbours to pass the time of day with, let alone the smell of the turf-fire of an evening! Homesick the poor boy was, and didn't know it.

The way it came about that Art left home was, he got tired of things there, the very things he wanted now. And there was some said, the mother was too good and fond with him. She'd lay the two hands under his feet any hour of the day or night; thought the sun shone out of him, so she did. And Art was always good and biddable with her; never gave any back talk, or was contrary. But all the time he wanted to be himself. He was much like a colt kept in a stall, well fed and minded, but he wants to get out to stretch his legs in a long gallop all the time.

So there's why Art went off from Ardenoo to the Big Smoke, and got on the best ever you knew. He was very apprehensive about machinery, could understand it well, and got took on by a great high-up doctor to mind his motor for him. The old people were that proud when they heard of it.

"Sure it's on the Pig's Back Art is now, whatever!" they said. "With his good-lookin' pound a week!"

Wealth that sounded, away off in Ardenoo. But the sorra much spending there is in it in a city, where you're paying out for everything you want. Delia did the best she could with it, but it wouldn't do all she wanted.

Still, she pleased Art. Small and white in the face she was, as Mrs. Moloney had imagined her. Sewing she used to be, a bad life for a girl to be at it all day. But she flourished up well after getting married. And what Art had looked into, when he was courting, was the big, longing-looking dark eyes of her, and the gentle voice and ways, and the clouds of soft brown hair … well, sure every eye forms a beauty of its own. But Art might have done worse nor to marry Delia Fogarty that never asked to differ from a word he said, till the notion came up of they going to Ardenoo for the Christmas. When the letter asking them came, he near riz the roof off the house, the shout he gave, he was that delighted in himself to be going back home.

"But what's a trouble to you, Delia?" he says, when he had time to take notice that she wasn't looking as rejoiced as he expected, only sitting there with her eyes upon the child in her arms, "A body'd think you didn't care about going at all!" he says, half vexed.

"I … I'd like to go, Art," says Delia, "only I don't know do I want to go or not…. I … do you see …"

"Well … what?"

"Sure … maybe … how do I know will they like me or not! And me coat all wore … and … and, moreover, I never got to get a right sort of a hood for the child … or a cloak…."

"Och, what at all, girl dear!" says Art, that was so excited at the thought of getting home that nothing was a trouble to him. "Not like you! What else would they do! And the child … well, now, isn't it well we told them nothing about him, the way he'll be a surprise to them now? The fine big fellah that he is! Sure it would be a sin to go put any clothes on him at all, hiding the brave big legs of him!"

Delia had to laugh at that; and then Art went out and bought a grand sheet of notepaper with robins and red berries and "The Season's Compliments" at the top of it. And Delia wrote the letter upon this, because she could write real neat and nice. Art told her every word to say:

> "Dear Father and Mother," it began, "I have pleasure in taking up my pen to rite yous those few lines hopping they find yous in good health as they leave us at this present thank you and God. I would wish my love and best wishes to…" and there were so many to be remembered that Art told Delia to put in "all inquiring friends," and even shortened like that, the list hardly left room for saying, "and we will go home for the Christmas and is obliged for the kindness of asking and we will go by the last train Christmas Eve and let yous meet that with Ling-gerin' Death and the cart and we're bringing a Christmas box wid us that yous will be rejoiced to see so I will end those few lines from your
>
> Son and New Daughter."

When that letter was finished and posted, Delia made no more of an objection to going, only did the best she could, washing and mending her own little things and the baby's. But let her do her best and they were poor-looking little bits of duds! And many's the time, when Art was away, that she'd cry, and wish to herself that there was no such a place as Ardenoo on the face of this earthly world. But what could she do, only please Art!

Well, the very evening before they were to start for Ardenoo, didn't Art come home to her in great humour. "Look at here, Delia!" says he, with a big laugh. "See the fine handful of money," and he held it out to her, "that Himself is after giving me in a Christmas box! Now we'll do the thing in real style! Come along out now, before the shops shut, and we'll buy all before us!"

Well, if you were to see the two of them that night! The three, indeed, for Delia wouldn't ever leave the child, only took him with her. To see them looking in at the grand bright windows full of things, and going in, Delia half afraid, but Art as loud and outspoken as a lord, spending free as long as it lasted! To see him then going home with her and the child, and he all loaded down with parcels, and opened them all out, the minute they got back! All the things they bought out of that money! A pipe and tobacco for Michael; a lovely cake with "Merry Christmas" in pink sugar upon it, for Herself; the grandest of brown shoes and a hat and feather for Delia, and as for the baby! Delia could scarce believe her eyes, all they had got for him, things she had been wanting....

Art made her fit them all on, and when she held up the child to be admired, with the loveliest of a soft white shawl rolled round him, "He becomes it well," says Art, "and I suppose you think to make him look better nor he is, by all that finery!"

"Your mother'll think him terrible small," said Delia, looking very fretted again; but she kissed the baby, as much as to say, "Little I care what she thinks!"

She said nothing about that part of it, though, only looked up at Art with the beseeching eyes I mentioned before.

"Let that go round!" says Art; and he lifted the two of them in his arms and kissed them both. And then when he had let Delia go, says he, "Me mother is the smallest little crathureen herself, that ever you saw! So she needn't talk! And sure what can you expect from a child not a month old yet! And there's an ould saying and a true one, in Ardenoo, 'It's not always the big people that reaps the harvest!' and so by this boy of ours! We won't feel till he'll be working!"

"Working!" said Delia. And she unclasped the baby's fingers and kissed the tiny hands inside, that were as soft and pink as rose leaves, first one hand and then the other. She never thought that every hand, no matter how rough and strong, begins by being a baby's hand like the one she was after kissing.

"Ay, work!" says Art, very determined. "It would amaze you or any one that didn't know, the way the children grow up and get sense at Ardenoo! The way if the old people seemed wishful for us to stop at home with them, this little fellah of ours would soon … but whisht!" Before poor Delia had time to say a word one way or other about this iday, "Whisht! what's this at all! A telegram! for me!"

A telegram! Poor Delia turned gashly pale at the word, and hugged the child closer to her, as if she thought that little bit of an orange-coloured envelope might be going to do some destruction on her treasure.

Art read it slowly to himself, while his face grew as long as today and tomorrow; and says he, "Well, it can't be helped! The Master that's after getting a hurried call to the country and will want me to drive him … so I'll not be at read'ness to go…." He looked anxiously at Delia.

Not go to Ardenoo! Delia's heart leaped up.

"Sure, can't we stop where we are?" says she, with dancing eyes.

"Och, not at all!" says Art. "It wouldn't answer at all to be disappointing them. And besides, it's down that side he wants to go … some sick child … the Master I mean … I'll likely be at Ardenoo before you!"

"But, Art! … is it go wid meself? What will I do at all at all?" and Delia begins to cry.

"See here now," says Art, "don't be taking on, that way! You wouldn't have me disappoint the Master … after he being so good to us, too! The fine grand little clothes we're after getting!… You'll be as right as rain! Just wait till you're at Ardenoo, where every one knows me! Why, you'll be with friends, that very minute! And you wrote it in the letter yourself, what train to meet you at…. You wouldn't be fretting me mother and she thinking to have us for the Christmas … to make no mention of the child at all!"

"To be sure not!" says Delia. And she dried her eyes and said no more, only got ready and went off the next day with the little child, as smiling and gay as she could appear, waving her hand to Art that saw her off at the Broadstone station, and did all he could to put her in heart. But it's a long, long ways from the Big

Smoke to Ardenoo. Hours and hours it took that wet, wild day to get there. And Delia wasn't too well accustomed to trains and going about. She managed to keep the child warm and comforted all through, but when the train stopped at Ardenoo she was that tired and giddy herself, that she scarcely knew what she was doing or where she was to go.

She stood a minute on the platform, with the wind and rain beating down upon her, till it had her even more confused. And the day was nearly done, and no lamps lit yet. But she made out a porter and asked him, as Art had bid her, for Mr. Moloney's ass-cart.

"Moloney's ass and dray? Ay," says the man, "Big Michael was in the Town today at Melia's, and buying all before him, by what I hear. And not too long ago it was …"

"Would I … could I find him … where's that place you're after mentioning?" And Delia took a grip of the big hat, that the wind was getting at.

"Melia's shop? You can't miss it! There's ne'er another…. He should have left it by now … but let you go on along that road …" and he showed her where it lay, stretching off into the darkness, "and you'll overtake him, ready! That ass is middling slow!"

The man guessed who this was speaking to him, for they all had heard about Art and the wife being expected for the Christmas. And he had no call to tell her to go off like that. Big Michael was nigh-hand at home again by then. But he had a sup taken at that present, as often happens at Christmas. Only he was a bit "on," he'd never have put such an iday into Delia's head. To think of letting her start after Michael like that!

But poor Delia knew no better than to follow fool's advice; how could she? So she just asked some directions about the road, and then she changed the child from one arm to the other and faced out in the night and rain, and a wind that would blow the horns off a goose to overtake the ass-cart. Little she thought that it was back at the Crooked Boreen by then, near five good miles away!

For a while, she wasn't in too bad a heart at all. She was glad to be out of the train, and she was expecting every step to get some signs of Michael on in front. But the little light there was went altogether before long; quenched, like, by the great rain and the heavy clouds that hung low and dark in the skies. Delia began to feel it very lonesome! But she kept going on; what else could she do?

At this time, what she thought worst of was, that the wet was spoiling her good hat, after Art spending his money upon it, the way she could make some kind of appearance foreninst his mother and the neighbours. But what could she do to save it?

"The cut I'll be!" she thought. "All dreeped with rain!" And indeed the hat, with its grand feather all broken and draggled, was a poor-looking thing enough before she was halfways to the Crooked Boreen. As for the grand shoes with the high heels, they were like sponges upon her feet, and she slipping in them as she stumbled along through mud and gutter to her ankles.

But she kept going on! The baby lay warm and snug upon her heart. She managed to keep him sheltered, anyway! Now and then she'd stop and put her face down to his, to feel his sweet warm breath upon her cheek. Then she'd go on again. That ass-cart! If only she could catch it! Wouldn't it be Heaven to be taken off her aching feet and be carried along, herself and the child, with some one that knew the way, and not to be feeling lost, as she did now.

For by degrees that's what Delia had to think; she was lost. Still she struggled on, the poor little bet-down thing that she was; so tired that she kept moving at all only by clenching her teeth hard and saying out loud, "I must! I must! A nice thing it would be for Art to not find me when he gets home! I must keep going on! The baby would die if I was to lie down …" For that is what she was more inclined for than anything else.

The wind was coming in great gusts now, hindering her far worse than the rain. It caught her skirts like the sails of a ship; it snatched at her hat. She tried to hold it on, but a sudden strong blast came, just as she was shifting the child again in her arms. Like a spiteful hand, it tore the hat from her head and furled it away; and what could be done, to get it again, in the storm and darkness? Delia cried at first, thinking of the loss it was. But she minded nothing long, only the tiredness and that still she must keep going on.

Suddenly she began to sing to the child:

I laid my love in a cradley-bed,
    Lu lu lu lu la lay.
Little white love with a soft round head,
    Lu lu lu lu la lay.

Before she had it done, she thought to see a light a piece off from her. She made towards it. Out upon the bog itself she was now; and them that saw her tracks after, said one of the holy Angels must have been guiding her then, that she wasn't drownded, herself and the child, in a bog-hole. She slipped here and she fell there on the wet, rough ground; but she kept on till she reached the light. It was the Christmas Candle, in Michael's stable, burning there, mild and watchful.

Chapter IV

THE CRIB

WHILE ALL THIS WAS GOING on, Big Michael was sitting, snug and comfortable, in the chimney-corner, opposite the wife, and she knitting, knitting away still. Not a word was passing. She had Michael's supper ready for him, hot and tasty, the same as ever. But he had no *goo* for it. What did he care was it good or bad! How could he feel gay and riz up in himself, the way a body should at the Christmas, when he knew well Herself had been crying away while he had been down at the stable?

If only she'd cheer up! If only she'd agree to have the place dressed out, and the Crib and all the other little things done the same as ever! It would do herself good, and they might be having a happy Christmas after all, even if there was only the two of them there with themselves! But he said nothing. Big as Michael was, and little as the Woman was that owned him, it was she had the upper hand in the house. And good right, too; she being a very understanding person, and considered to be a good adviser of a woman all over Ardenoo. Michael was slow, but he was wise enough to give in to the wife. So now when she showed no wish for any of the things he was so made upon, he said no more about them; only after a while says he, "I believe it's what I'll take a streel off to see is the cow all right in the stable below...."

But what he really wanted was, to get away from the queer, unhappy feel of the silent kitchen. He thought, too, he'd like another sight of the dressed-out stable and the big Candle he had lit there. He meant to stop a bit with those Christmas signs, and the ass, and the munch, munch of the cow, filling the place with her fragrant breath.

Wasn't it a pity of the world that Herself was having none of the pleasure? If only he could tell her what he had been doing! If only he could get her to come, too, and see how lovely the stable looked!

As he passed out on the door, the Vanithee looked after him. A kind of pity rose warm in her heart, as she saw the fretted appearance was upon the big man, like a cowed dog, with his tail drooping between his legs.

All the bygone Christmas Eves they had put in there together! Kind, pleasant times, with little old nonsense and laughing, that no one understood, only themselves! Art had been there, to be sure! He had been the delight of the first of their Christmases, and the same always, till he went off. But was it Michael's fault that the son wasn't there yet? Sure poor Michael had done nothing to fret her! It wasn't he had neglected to write! And wasn't it full as bad for him, Michael, that had always been the fond father to Art! And had never rightly overed the boy's quitting off the way he did! Oh, if only they had Art there again! To have him going off with the father of a morning, cutting turf, or making hay, or doing a bit of ploughing, and the two of them in to their dinners and off again!... Why, to have that good time back, she'd even welcome the poor-lookin' little scollop of a thing, and give her share of the old home!...

Poor Michael! He that loved the Christmas! Like a child, he was! Most men are, if they have any good in them; and God help them if they get a woman that doesn't understand that, and can't make allowances when they don't grow up!

Mrs. Moloney was as quick as Michael was slow. So, while he'd be thinking about it, she had a stool over at the dresser and was up on it, feeling for the Crib on the top shelf.

It was there, safe enough, and it wrapped in a newspaper. A small little contraption of a thing it was, that she had bought off Tommy the Crab, the peddling man, years before. Paid sixpence for it, too; and cheap he told her it was at that money.

To see it first, it was no more than a middling sizeable Christmas card. But it was really in three, or maybe four, halves that drew out like a telescope. The first part showed the Kings kneeling with their offerings and crowns upon their heads; then you could see the Shepherds, with their crooks and they kneeling, too; and in the middle of them all, the Mother herself, with the Holy Child upon her knee. St. Joseph was at one side, and the ox and the ass at the other; all complete, even to a grand Star of silver paper, shining on the top of it all.

Mrs. Moloney put the Crib into one of the small square windows and drew it out. Then she went back to the dresser for the candles to light it up with. It looked nothing wanting them.

Not common candles she was going to use, but what had been blessed at Candlemas, and that she had kept put by very carefully.

"I mustn't take them all," she thought, "the way, if one of us was to take and die sudden, there would be a Candle ready to put into the dying hand, to light the soul on its way! But there's a good few, and so …"

Four she took for the four evangelists, and was just lighting them up, when suddenly the door burst open, and with a rush and a laugh in came … Art!

"Mother!" he said; and in a moment had his arms round her, and was kissing her lips.

"Oh, Art! So you did come, after all!" says she, with a catch in her breath and a gush of joy to her heart. She had her son, her own son again! And for a minute she forgot everything else—the missed letter, Art's wife….

"Come? And why wouldn't I come? What else? Och, but it's grand, the smell of the turf! And the Crib the same as ever! Och, mother, mother! But where's Delia? Some tricks you and her is up to! Has them hid 'on' me? Delia! Delia! Where at all are you?"

At that the mother drew a piece away from him. Her face that had been smiling and rosy even, like a girl's face, grew stiff and white.

"Delia! Delia! He can think of nothing else," she thought. It all came back upon her, like a bad dream. Her son had a wife now! And she had held out her hand to them, and they had slighted it!

What did Art mean, coming in like a strong wind? Gay and pleasant as summer air at first, but his face changed and became black and stormy and his voice was a strange, fierce voice, asking again, "Where's Delia?"

"I know nothing about her! How could I?"

"Sure she was to be here …"

"We got no word …"

"No word! Is it that no one met them at the train? My God! What has become of her and the child? And the night it was!"

The child? What child? the mother was trying to ask, but the words were stopped on her lips, and Art was stopped at the door, in his mad rush forth to look for his wife and baby, by the appearance before them of Michael. Stopped them both, I say, but without a word being spoken. It was just the look in the old man's face that made them both fall back a step and stand still, looking at Michael in a sort of wonder and fright. His eyes were shining, as if he had been in another world, and had scarcely got back to earth again. He stood facing them for a minute with the same far away look; then he took each of them by the hand, and just breathed out, "Come! come with me and see what's in the stable …"

They went. The wind had fallen and the rain had ceased. A beautiful moon had risen, and was shining, but you could not see her, only the light she shed down from her throne on high through the soft white mist that had risen from the wet ground and was wavering and dancing solemnly to and fro, filling the space between heaven and earth, as if to veil the sacred sights of the Holy Eve from mortal eyes. The father and mother and son moved silently through the misty, gleaming silence, till they reached the stable, where the Candle was burning steadily, and sending forth its pure white light into the moonlit vapour.

Michael stepped on and was at the door first. He put his great arm across, as if to ensure caution and reverence.

"Go easy, go easy, the both of yous! But sure, they might be gone back already, and no one to have seen them, only meself!" he said in the same awed whisper.

They peered in, for beyond the Candle were dusky spaces; yet its light was enough to show them two figures there; a girl-mother with her child, lying very still.

Was she asleep, or…. She was so white and small! The long dark hair had been loosened and fell about her like a soft mantle; and close, close to her heart lay the little child.

"Delia, Delia!" said Art.

"The Child!" said his mother.

Delia unclosed her eyes and looked up with a little smile. "I have him here, safe!" she said.

And Michael, only half comprehending, fell on his knees and sobbed aloud.

The Troubles at Christmas

BERNARD MACLAVERTY

THE NEXT DAY WAS THURSDAY and despite the snow and the state of the roads he went into town early with Dunlop to do his Christmas shopping. He wondered what he could buy for Marcella—something that wouldn't attract questions. Not that he could afford much. He bought her a tiny bottle of perfume which cost him the best part of three days' wages and in a bookshop he asked if they had any books by or about the artist who had so impressed her. The assistant gave him a small paperback of Grünewald's paintings and he slipped it into his pocket. He bought Shamie a bottle of aftershave and a shaving stick, as he had done every year since he could remember. They seemed to last exactly from Christmas to Christmas. He also bought his father a one-thousand-piece jigsaw to cheer him up. When Cal was a child Shamie had always interfered over his shoulder, wanting to put pieces into his jigsaws. In the toy shop he saw some "Raggedy Ann" dolls flopped against the wall with their heads pitched forward like drunks. He bought one for Lucy.

Outside, the Preacher stood at the corner shouting at the top of his voice about God. He wore a black plastic apron with the words "Repent ye; for the Kingdom of Heaven is at hand." There was no one listening to him except a few of his cronies, also wearing black bibs, who were standing up against the wall. Everyone else bustled past, some even stepping into the slush of the gutter to avoid him. He windmilled his arms and shouted as Cal passed him.

"Without the shedding of blood there can be no forgiveness."

"Good evening," said Cal.

He got no answer from Dermot Ryan's front door so he went round the back and found it open. He went in, kicking the snow off his shoes, and called for Shamie but there was no answer. He sat down to wait. Perhaps they had both gone out for a drink. If they had, it was a good sign. He took out the paperback of the paintings and began to look through it. He heard the front door open and shouted a warning that he was in. Dermot opened the door by himself.

"Where's Shamie?"

"He was worse than they thought, Cal. The doctor put him in for treatment."

"Where?"

"Gransha."

"Oh God, no."

"They say this electrical shock treatment is bad. Very hard on you."

"How the hell am I supposed to get to Derry to see him?"

Dermot shrugged and sat down, readjusting his cap on his head. Briefly Cal saw the track of the headband on the little hair that Dermot had.

"What about the van? Where is it?"

"A boy at the abattoir has it."

"Crilly?"

"Aye, I think so."

"Jesus."

"Too generous for his own good. He's some man, your father. It broke my heart to see the way he was. Like iron to Plasticine overnight." He sat close to the fire, the top buttons of his trousers undone making a white V on his potbelly. One hand was on his knee, the other hooked in his braces.

"Cal, the world is full of gulpins who don't care who they hurt."

"Will he be out for Christmas?"

"I doubt it—from what the doctor said."

Cal went over to the table where he had left the presents.

"If you see him, will you give him this?" he said and handed the large box to Dermot. "And there's a present for yourself for putting up with him." He gave Dermot the wrapped after-shave and stick. "It's the same brand as Shamie uses and I got to like the smell of it."

"Thanks, Cal. You're as like your father as two peas in a pod."

He went to the library to pass the time and was disappointed and annoyed when he saw the bespectacled figure of the head librarian behind the desk instead of Marcella. If he had thought about it for a moment he would have realized that with nobody to mind her child in the evening she would not be on duty. Now he would have to walk home, or hitchhike, which was dangerous.

He wandered down to the section which had the cartoon books and opened one—a selection from *The New Yorker*. A voice behind him said,

"Good to see you, Cal."

He froze and without looking he knew it was Crilly.

"I didn't expect to see you in a place like this," said Cal, turning to face him. The big man stood smiling, his head hanging to make him look less tall.

"Why not?"

"I read one book in school. That was one more than you."

"The books is not for me. Here, c'mere."

He led Cal over to the fiction section and cocked his head to the side. He ran his finger along the titles and tapped a fat book. *Middlemarch* by George Eliot. Cal said, "So what?"

"There's plenty in that book," said Crilly. He took it out very gently and looked all around him and, seeing no one, flipped open the cover. There was a square hole cut in the pages. Inside was a small bag of powder wired to a watch. Crilly closed the book carefully and slipped it back onto the shelf. He said,

"I don't borrow books. I bring them in."

"Jesus, why do you want to burn down a library?"

"Government property, in't it? Orders is orders, Cal."

"Fuckin' hell."

Cal turned away from him but Crilly gripped his arm.

"Skeffington would like a word with you." He added, "Urgent."

"I'm not interested anymore."

"We've been looking all over for you. I heard you were in England."

"No, I'm still around."

Crilly's hand remained on his arm.

"Where?"

"Here."

The librarian looked over his glasses to see who was speaking so loudly. Crilly smiled and reduced his voice to a whisper close to Cal's ear.

"Now, Cal, don't fuck me about. Where are you living at?"

"Outside town."

"Let's go to my house and Skeffington can drop in and see us, eh?"

Cal shrugged. Crilly's voice had turned friendly but Cal knew that he shouldn't go. He allowed himself to be led out of the library and onto the street. Crilly walked very close to him. He asked him what was in the parcel and Cal told him it was a doll. Cal thought of running but it seemed so stupid to run away from this guy he had been to school with.

"Too bad about Shamie. How is he?" asked Crilly.

"He's away in Gransha."

"Yes. I know. He lent me the van."

"You mean you took it."

"Sort of."

"I want it back. Like now."

"It's being used, Cal."

"Soon, then. I have to get out to Gransha to see him."

"I've never seen such a change in a man. Did you hear about Skeffington's father?"

"The wit? Don't tell me he spoke."

"He got knocked down by a car."

"Bad?"

"Bad enough. Just a minute."

Crilly stopped at the phone box at the end of the street and opened the door for Cal. The two men stood with their knees almost touching while Crilly dialled. Cal heard the receiver burr three times, then Crilly put it back. Cal was about to push open the door to leave when Crilly said, "Wait." They waited and the phone rang three times and stopped.

"Neat?" said Crilly. "Saves money. Saves phone tapping."

"It's a wonder the phone is in order."

"It's in order because we want it to be in order. A bit of discipline around the district works wonders."

In Crilly's front room they sat waiting for Skeffington. There was an electric clock on the narrow mantelpiece with a sweep second hand which made slow progress round the face. Cal thought of the watch in the darkness of a closed book in Marcella's library. He did not dare ask Crilly what time it was set for but he guessed it would be well after closing time. Incendiaries could be put out if they went off when the staff were still there. Cal said, "You were telling me about witty old Skeffington."

"Oh, aye. He got knocked down by this drunken bastard of about sixteen. The wee shite had *stolen* the car. He fractured the old man's skull and broke both his legs. Christ, was Skeffington mad. He spent all night at the hospital and when I saw him the next day he was biting the table. He said he wanted an example made of this lad. I've never done a knee capping but, says I, 'I'll have a go.' Says he, 'I'll drive for you. I want to see this one myself. And what's more,' says he, 'don't use a gun—get the captive bolt from work. I don't want this guy to walk again for a long time.' Wallop, wallop. Both knees he wanted, and your man on the ground squealing like a stuck pig with Skeffington sitting on his head."

Cal said, "That was stupid."

"Why?"

"They'll be able to tell what made that wound."

"Jesus, I hadn't thought of that."

"An entry wound with no exit and no bullets? They'll trace it back."

"Jesus, you're right." Crilly scratched the top of his head. "Cal, you should have stuck with us."

Mrs. Crilly looked into the room and, seeing Cal, bared her white dentures in a smile.

"Hello, Cal," she said. "Tea or coffee?"

"He'll wait for Finbar, Ma. He should be along any second."

When he came Skeffington didn't shake hands with Cal as he usually did but spoke to him across the room. He seemed serious and anxious.

"I believe we share a problem, Cahal."

"What's that?"

"Our fathers being ill."

"Yes. How is yours?"

"They tell me he'll live. But broken bones at that age … He'll never be the same again."

"I'm sorry."

Skeffington sat down in the armchair. He turned to speak to Crilly.

"Well?"

"Easy. No bother," said Crilly. "That's where I met our friend here." Cal tried to remember the name of the man who wrote the book. When Skeffington spoke to Cal his voice sounded deeply hurt.

"Cahal, why didn't you let us know where you were?"

"I told you before. I want out."

"Sometimes there's a price to pay."

"Yeah, I was just telling him," said Crilly, "about what we did to your friend last night."

"Sometimes," said Skeffington to Crilly, "you are extremely stupid."

"I was just trying to put him in the mood for listening to you. And it was *your* stupid idea to use the humane killer on him. Cal says they'll be able to trace it."

"Highly unlikely. Have you not realized yet that Cahal is no longer on our side? He should be told nothing. Cahal has had a change of heart, isn't that so?"

"I don't think I've changed all that much. I see things differently now."

"That's what's called becoming a traitor to the cause. The next step is to become an informer." Skeffington still had his overcoat and scarf on and held his left leather glove in his gloved right hand. He lay back in the chair, sighing. "I really thought better of you, Cahal. In its fight for Irish freedom this kind of thing has dogged the Republican Movement all through the centuries. Our own Lundys have thrown it away—nameless rats from Ireland's sad past."

"I have not informed on anybody," said Cal. "I just felt bad about what I was doing. It was against my conscience. Was it you guys who planted the mine out on the Toome road?"

"No. That must have been the lads from Ballyronan. Why?"

"They killed a cow."

"That kind of sarcasm helps no one, Cahal. Mistakes are inevitable."

"You mean it would have been all right if it had been a person?"

"Did you ever hear of Archbishop Romero? He talked about the 'legitimate right of insurrectional violence.' Oppressed peoples have the *right* to throw off the yoke in whatever way they see fit—and that's from an eminent doctor of the Church. If somebody is standing on your neck you have the right to break his leg."

"With a captive bolt?"

"Yes. If it will be a lesson to others. There are no rules, Cahal. Just eventual winners. I myself prefer the God of the Old Testament: 'You who strike all my foes on the mouth, you who break the teeth of the wicked.'"

Mrs. Crilly came smiling in again with her wobbling tin tray.

"It's bitter outside. Would you not turn on the other bar of that fire?" She set the tray on the table and asked Skeffington about his father, listening to what was said with concern.

"Och well, he'll be warm in the hospital tonight. The central heating in those places would boil you. I think it's why the half of them die. That couldn't be good for you. When I was in for my hysterectomy—I've had the whole works removed, y'know—the sweat was breaking on me the whole time. The doctor said it might just be the change of life but I thought it was the central heating."

"Thanks, Ma," said Crilly, holding the door open for her. When she had gone Cal lifted his cup and blew on his tea. There was an awkward silence. Cal looked at the clock. The library would be closed by now. He remembered the noise of the fire in his own house, the thunderous roaring of the flames. He thought of Marcella the next day tramping on the broken glass and the wet charred floor, looking at the remains of her library, the stink of destruction in her nose. The only books in Crilly's house were a set of four bound *Reader's Digest*s—green spines with gold lettering—held upright by a plaster dog at each end. In the middle. Remember in the middle of March—a month of the year.

"Well, Cahal?"

"What's this price you're talking of?"

"We want to know where you are staying—so's we can get in touch with you if we need you."

"So the price of getting out is staying in?"

"More or less."

"And if I refuse?"

"Cahal, look. I have been extremely lenient with you up until now. This is not a game we're playing. What you have done is called desertion. You know the penalties for that in any other army in wartime."

Crilly stood up and walked behind Cal. Cal watched him out of the corner of his eye. He held tightly on to his parcel.

"But look. I keep telling you I never joined. I helped out once or twice ..."

There was a long silence. Skeffington separated the fingers of his limp glove. Crilly looked through the curtains and made a slurping noise as he drank his tea. Cal heard the characteristic sound of a Land Rover engine outside and was aware of Crilly stiffening. A door slammed and Crilly hissed.

"It's the fuckin' cops."

Skeffington jumped to his feet.

"Out the back."

They moved quickly into the hall. The bell rang and almost before it had ceased the door was hammered by a fist. They saw a peaked cap at the bubbled oval of glass. In the back room Crilly's mother and father were sitting watching television in blue darkness and Skeffington told them not to answer the door for a while. The three of them slipped out of the back door into the small snowy garden. Cal was in the middle as they went crunching down the path. Suddenly a voice shouted "Halt!" and Cal glimpsed a peaked R.U.C. cap rise above the hedge at the bottom of the garden. Skeffington stopped dead. Cal took one step to the side. Between the toolshed and the coal house there was a gap of about a foot. Crilly tried to follow him but a voice screamed again, "Halt or I fire." Crilly stood still. Cal heard his own clothes scrape and brush between the walls. His paper bag crackled so he quickly pulled the doll out and dropped the paper onto the ground. He held his breath and stepped up on a wire which separated him from the next door garden. It twanged with his weight. He crept behind some bushes, terrified he would be seen against the whiteness of the snow, then through the hedge on hands and knees to the next garden. He heard angry voices from Crilly's. The houses were in terraces of four and there was a way onto the street from this garden. Doubled over. Cal made it away from the backs and stood at the front gate looking into the street. Others had come to their doors and were standing watching the Land Rover. Somebody shouted an obscenity at the policeman sitting at the wheel and a snowball bounced hollowly off its roof. The snowball was followed by stones. Cal walked away from the street as casually as he could onto the main road, carrying the Raggedy Ann like a baby against his shoulder.

On the corner next to the post office there was a telephone box and Cal went into it and set the doll on the shelf. It slumped forward, staring at its knees. The number of the Confidential Phone was framed on the wall but somebody had rubbed either mud or shit over it to obscure it. He made it out and dialled. He told the voice at the other end that there was a fire bomb in the library and that it was in a book called *Middlemarch* by somebody called Eliot. No, he didn't know whether it was the only one. He put the phone down as if it was a black garden slug and left the box. Skeffington was right. He had turned informer.

It took him over an hour to walk home beneath a sky that was clear of cloud and thick with stars. Twice he saw shooting stars score the sky momentarily. It was freezing cold, and to keep himself warm he walked quickly and rhythmically in the black scar at the centre of the road which had been cleared of snow. There were few cars and at this time of night none stopped to give him a lift. He wondered if either Crilly or Skeffington would crack and give them Cal's name. How long did they question you? Did they kick the living daylights out of you, as he'd heard? Or did they just break you by keeping you awake and persistence? He'd heard of one trick they'd used, of blindfolding the guy and putting him in a helicopter, but taking him up only about two feet, then chucking him out. Or ball squeezing – hurting you in ways that didn't show afterwards. He felt sure that Skeffington would never break. Crilly on the other hand was not too bright and anybody could tie him in knots.

When he turned the bend in the road his first reaction was to look towards the farmhouse and, seeing a light on downstairs, he broke into a run. He rang the bell and heard Marcella ask, "Who is it?"

"It's Cal."

The door opened. She was in her nightdress and dressing gown and when he passed her in the doorway she smelt clean and washed.

"Where were you? I went down to the cottage and you weren't there."

"I was in town. I thought you'd be in the library," he said. "I had to walk it home." The doll was beneath the crook of his arm and he offered it to her for Lucy, apologizing for the lack of wrapping. She thanked him extravagantly and they stood awkwardly facing each other. He unzipped his anorak and stood with his back to the fire. She smiled and after a moment's hesitation slid her arms around him inside his anorak and laid her head against his shirt front and thumping heart.

"I feel the cold off you," she said.

He smelt the soft hair of the top of her head and kissed it, held her as if to crush her. He wanted to tell her that he had saved her precious library but knew it would be too complicated. He wanted to be open and honest with her and tell her everything. To explain how the events of his life were never what he wanted, how he seemed unable to influence what was going on around him. He had had a recurring dream of sitting at the wheel of a car driving and at a critical point turning the wheel and nothing happening. For miles the car would career along with the steering wheel, slack, and he would spin it round and round like a ship's wheel but nothing would happen. Eventually he would hit something—a wall, another vehicle; once he woke roaring in his throat after seeing a child with bright amazed eyes disappearing beneath the front of the car and feeling the bounce of wheels on flesh and bone.

"Comfort me, Cal," she said.

He stepped back and pulled the tie of her dressing gown. He put his hands beneath and round her shoulders. He felt the warm lines of her body through the thin material. He caressed her from neck to knee, feeling no interruption to the smooth passage of his hands. And they made love in an absolute and intense silence.

"Tomorrow they come back," she said, "and my life will just become a fragment of theirs again."

"Why don't you leave? Get a flat and I can come and visit you."

"Yes, that sounds so easy. I've told her that many times. I wish I wasn't so weak. I wish I could fight with her and insult her. But when it comes to a crisis she always wins. The only way I could do it is not be here when they get back. It's been a year now, and every time I tell her I'm moving something comes up and she persuades me to stay on. For Lucy's sake. For Grandad's sake. After Easter."

Cal told her about his own father having to go in to hospital.

"And at Christmas," she said. "Cal, you must come here for Christmas dinner. It would be a relief for me to have someone to talk to. And it could seem as if I'm acting out of charity. Will you do that for me?"

Cal nodded and yet he had the feeling he would never be there. So much so that he crawled naked to where he had flung his anorak on the chair and gave her Christmas presents.

"Can I open them now?" she said. "I can never wait."

She touched between her breasts with the perfume and kissed him. Then in the book she sought and found Grünewald's picture of Christ crucified and held it up for Cal to see. The weight of the Christ figure bent the cross down like a bow; the hands were cupped to heaven like nailed starfish; the body with its taut rib cage was pulled to the shape of an egg timer by the weight of the lower body; the flesh was diseased with sores from the knotted scourges, the mouth open and gasping for breath. She was sitting on the floor with her back to the couch, her legs open in a yoga position and the book facing him, just below her breasts. Cal looked at the flesh of Christ spotted and torn, bubonic almost, and then behind it at the smoothness of Marcella's body and it became a permanent picture in his mind.

They ate supper and went to her bed to make love again and she made Cal promise to leave before morning to avoid the attentions of Lucy when she woke. Marcella lay, her bottom snug in the cup of his thighs and belly and talked. The pauses grew longer until eventually she stopped altogether. Her breathing became deep and regular and her leg jerked in a dream. Cal lay awake beside her, touching her bare back with his cheek. The trust she showed in falling asleep beside him made him feel worse. Could he *ever* tell her the truth? Perhaps he could write it down. That way he could say what he meant and not get confused. He could write to her and if she replied he could begin to hope. But would she tell the police? A letter of confession would be evidence that would put him away for most of his life. She was what he wanted most and if he couldn't be near her he might as well be in prison. If he was ever caught—and there was an impending sense that it wouldn't be long now that Crilly and Skeffington were lifted—he would write to her and try to tell it as it was. He had her now like the Sleeping Beauty of his fantasy. He reached out his hand and touched her moistness but she grumbled in her sleep and jackknifed, closing him out. He kissed the nape of her neck, got up and dressed in the darkness.

Walking back to the cottage he heard the sounds of a thaw. The black lane showed through the centres of footsteps when the moon raced from one cloud to the next. The air had warmed and melted snow was running down the sides of the lane. Everywhere was the sound of dripping and clinking and gurgling.

The next morning, Christmas Eve, almost as if he expected it, the police arrived to arrest him and he stood in a dead man's Y-fronts listening to the charge, grateful that at last someone was going to beat him to within an inch of his life.

Men and Women

CLAIRE KEEGAN

MY FATHER TAKES ME PLACES. He has artificial hips, so he needs me to open gates. To reach our house you must drive up a long lane through a wood, open two sets of gates and close them behind you so the sheep won't escape to the road. I'm handy. I get out, open the gates, my father freewheels the Volkswagen through, I close the gates behind him and hop back into the passenger seat. To save petrol he starts the car on the run, gathering speed on the slope before the road, and then we're off to wherever my father is going on that particular day.

Sometimes it's the scrap yard, where he's looking for a spare part, or, scenting a bargain in some classified ad, we wind up in a farmer's mucky field, pulling cabbage plants or picking seed potatoes in a dusty shed. Sometimes we drive to the forge, where I stare into the water barrel, whose surface reflects patches of the milky skies that drift past, sluggish, until the blacksmith plunges the red-hot metal down and scorches away the clouds. On Saturdays my father goes to the mart and examines sheep in the pens, feeling their backbones, looking into their mouths. If he buys just a few sheep, he doesn't bother going home for the trailer but puts them in the back of the car, and it is my job to sit between the front seats to keep them there. They shit small pebbles and say *baaaah*, the Suffolks' tongues dark as the raw liver we cook on Mondays. I keep them back until we get to whichever house Da stops at for a feed on the way home. Usually it's Bridie

Knox's, because Bridie kills her own stock and there's always meat. The hand brake doesn't work, so when Da parks in her yard I get out and put the stone behind the wheel.

I am the girl of a thousand uses.

"Be the holy, missus, what way are ya?"

"Dan!" Bridie says, like she didn't hear the splutter of the car.

Bridie lives in a smoky little house without a husband, but she has sons who drive tractors around the fields. They're small, deeply unattractive men who patch their Wellingtons. Bridie wears red lipstick and face powder, but her hands are like a man's hands. I think her head is wrong for her body, the way my dolls look when I swap their heads.

"Have you aer a bit for the child, missus? She's hungry at home," Da says, looking at me like I'm one of those African children we give up sugar for during Lent.

"Ah now," says Bridie, smiling at his old joke. "That girl looks fed to me. Sit down there and I'll put the kettle on."

"To tell you the truth, missus, I wouldn't fall out with a drop of something. I'm after being in at the mart and the price of sheep is a holy scandal."

He talks about sheep and cattle and the weather and how this little country of ours is in a woeful state while Bridie sets the table, puts out the Chef sauce and the Colman's mustard and cuts big, thick slices off a flitch of beef or boiled ham. I sit by the window and keep an eye on the sheep, who stare, bewildered, from the car. Da eats everything in sight while I build a little tower of biscuits and lick the chocolate off and give the rest to the sheepdog under the table.

When we get home, I find the fire shovel and collect the sheep-droppings from the car and roll barley on the loft.

"Where did you go?" Mammy asks.

I tell her all about our travels while we carry buckets of calf-nuts and beet-pulp across the yard. Da sits in under the shorthorn cow and milks her into a bucket. My brother sits in the sitting room beside the fire and pretends he's studying. He will do the Intercert. next year. My brother is going to be somebody, so he doesn't open gates or clean up shite or carry buckets. All he does is read and write and draw triangles with special pencils Da buys him for mechanical drawing. He is the brains in the family. He stays in there until he is called to dinner.

"Go down and tell Seamus his dinner is on the table," Da says.

I have to take off my Wellingtons before I go down.

"Come up and get it, you lazy fucker," I say.

"I'll tell," he says.

"You won't," I say, and go back up to the kitchen, where I spoon garden peas onto his plate because he won't eat turnip or cabbage like the rest of us.

Evenings, I get my schoolbag and do homework on the kitchen table while Ma watches the television we hire for winter. On Tuesdays she makes a big pot of tea before eight o'clock and sits at the range and glues herself to the programme where a man teaches a woman how to drive a car. How to change gears, to let the clutch out and give her the juice. Except for a rough woman up behind the hill who drives a tractor and a Protestant woman in the town, no woman we know drives. During the break her eyes leave the screen and travel with longing to the top shelf of the dresser, where she has hidden the spare key to the Volkswagen in the old cracked teapot. I am not supposed to know this. I sigh and continue tracing the course of the River Shannon through a piece of greaseproof paper.

ON CHRISTMAS EVE I PUT up signs. I cut up a cardboard box and in red marker I write THIS WAY SANTA and arrows pointing the way. I am always afraid he will get lost or not bother coming because the gates are too much trouble. I staple them onto the paling at the end of the lane and on the timber gates and one inside the door leading down to the parlour where the tree is. I put a glass of stout and a piece of cake on the coffee table for him and conclude that Santa must be drunk by Christmas morning.

Daddy takes his good hat out of the press and looks at himself in the mirror. It's a fancy hat with a stiff feather stuck down in the brim. He tightens it well down on his head to hide his bald patch.

"And where are you going on Christmas Eve?" Mammy asks.

"Going off to see a man about a pup," he says, and bangs the door.

I go to bed and have trouble sleeping. I am the only person in my class Santa Claus still visits. I know this because the master asked, "Who does Santa Claus still come to?" and mine was the only hand raised. I'm different, but every year I feel there is a greater chance that he will not come, that I will become like the others.

I wake at dawn and Mammy is already lighting the fire, kneeling on the hearth, ripping up newspaper, smiling. There is a terrible moment when I think maybe Santa didn't come because I said "Come and get it, you lazy fucker," but he does come. He leaves me the Tiny Tears doll I asked for, wrapped in the same wrapping paper we have, and I think how the postal system is like magic, how I can send a letter two days before Christmas and it reaches the North Pole overnight, even though it takes a week for a letter to reach England. Santa does not come to Seamus any more. I suspect he knows what Seamus is really doing all those evenings in the sitting room, reading *Hit n Run* magazines and drinking the red lemonade out of the sideboard, not using his brains at all.

Nobody's up except Mammy and me. We are the early birds. We make tea, eat toast and chocolate fingers for breakfast. Then she puts on her best apron, the one with all the strawberries, and turns on the radio, chops onions and parsley while I grate a plain loaf into crumbs. We stuff the turkey and waltz around the kitchen. Seamus and Da come down and investigate the parcels under the tree. Seamus gets a dartboard for Christmas. He hangs it on the back door and himself and Da throw darts and chalk up scores while Mammy and me put on our anoraks and feed the pigs and cattle and sheep and let the hens out.

"How come they do nothing?" I ask her. I am reaching into warm straw, feeling for eggs. The hens lay less in winter.

"They're men," she says, as if this explains everything.

Because it is Christmas morning, I say nothing. I come inside and duck when a dart flies past my head.

"Ha! Ha!" says Seamus.

"Bulls-eye," says Da.

ON NEW YEAR'S EVE IT snows. Snowflakes land and melt on the window ledges. It is the end of another year. I eat a bowl of sherry trifle for breakfast and fall asleep watching *Lassie* on TV. I play with my dolls after dinner but get fed up filling Tiny Tears with water and squeezing it out through the hole in her backside, so I take her head off, but her neck is too thick to fit onto my other dolls' bodies. I start playing darts with Seamus. He chalks two marks on the lino, one for him and another, closer to the board, for me. When I get a treble nineteen, Seamus says, "Fluke."

"Eighty-seven," I say, totting up my score.

"Fluke," he says.

"You don't know what fluke is," I say. "Fluke and worms. Look it up in the dictionary."

"Exactly," he says.

I am fed up being treated like a child. I wish I was big. I wish I could sit beside the fire and be called up to dinner and draw triangles, lick the nibs of special pencils, sit behind the wheel of a car and have someone open gates that I could drive through. *Vrum! Vrum!* I'd give her the holly, make a bumper sticker that would read: CAUTION, SHEEP ON BOARD.

That night we get dressed up. Mammy wears a dark red dress, the colour of the shorthorn cow. Her skin is freckled like somebody dipped a toothbrush in paint and splattered her. She asks me to fasten the catch on her string of pearls. I used to stand on the bed doing this, but now I'm tall, the tallest girl in my class; the master measured us. Mammy is tall and thin, but the skin on her hands is hard. I wonder if someday she will look like Bridie Knox, become part man, part woman.

Da does not do himself up. I have never known him to take a bath or wash his hair; he just changes his hat and shoes. Now he clamps his good hat down on his head and puts his shoes on. They are big black shoes he bought when he sold the Suffolk ram. He has trouble with the laces, as he finds it hard to stoop. Seamus wears a green jumper with elbow patches, black trousers with legs like tubes and cowboy boots to make him taller.

"You'll trip up in your high heels," I say.

We get into the Volkswagen, me and Seamus in the back and Mammy and Da up front. Even though I washed the car out, I can smell sheep-shite, a faint, pungent odour that always drags us back to where we come from. I resent this deeply. Da turns on the windscreen wiper; there's only one, and it screeches as it wipes the snow away. Crows rise from the trees, releasing shrill, hungry sounds. Because there are no doors in the back, it is Mammy who gets out to open the gates. I think she is beautiful with her pearls around her throat and her red skirt flaring out when she swings round. I wish my father would get out, that the snow would be falling on him, not on my mother in her good clothes. I've seen other fathers holding their wives' coats, holding doors open, asking if they'd like anything at the shop, bringing home bars of chocolate and ripe pears even when they say no. But Da's not like that.

Spellman Hall stands in the middle of a car park, an arch of bare, multicoloured bulbs surrounding a crooked "Merry Christmas" sign above the door. Inside is big as a warehouse with a slippy wooden floor and benches at the walls. Strange lights make every white garment dazzle. It's amazing. I can see the newsagent's bra through her blouse, fluff like snow on the auctioneer's trousers. The accountant has a black eye and a jumper made of grey and white wool diamonds. Overhead a globe of shattered mirror shimmers and spins slowly. At the top of the ballroom a Formica-topped table is stacked with bottles of lemonade and orange, custard-cream biscuits and cheese-and-onion Tayto. The butcher's wife stands behind, handing out the straws and taking in the money. Several of the women I know from my trips around the country are there: Bridie with her haw-red lipstick; Sarah Combs, who only last week urged my father to have a glass of sherry and gave me stale cake while she took him into the sitting room to show him her new suite of furniture; Miss Emma Jenkins, who always makes a fry and drinks coffee instead of tea and never has a sweet thing in the house because of her gastric juices.

On the stage men in red blazers and candy-striped bowties play drums, guitars, blow horns, and The Nerves Moran is out front, singing "My Lovely Leitrim." Mammy and I are first out on the floor for the cuckoo waltz, and when the music stops, she dances with Seamus. My father dances with the women from the roads. I wonder how he can dance like that and not open gates. Seamus jives with teenage girls he knows from the vocational school, hand up, arse out and the girls spinning like blazes. Old men in their thirties ask me out.

"Will ya chance a quickstep?" they say. Or: "How's about a half-set?"

They tell me I'm light on my feet.

"Christ, you're like a feather," they say, and put me through my paces.

In the Paul Jones the music stops and I get stuck with a farmer who smells sour like the whiskey we make sick lambs drink in springtime, but the young fella who hushes the cattle around the ring in the mart butts in and rescues me.

"Don't mind him," he says. "He thinks he's the bee's knees."

He smells of ropes, new galvanise, Jeyes Fluid.

After the half-set I get thirsty and Mammy gives me a fifty-pence piece for lemonade and raffle tickets. A slow waltz begins and Da walks across to Sarah Combs, who rises from the bench and takes her jacket off. Her shoulders are bare; I can see the top of her breasts. Mammy is sitting with her handbag on her lap, watching. There is something sad about Mammy tonight; it is all around her like when a cow dies and the truck comes to take it away. Something I don't fully understand is happening, as if a black cloud has drifted in and could burst and cause havoc. I go over and offer her my lemonade, but she just takes a little, dainty sip and thanks me. I give her half my raffle tickets, but she doesn't care. My father has his arms around Sarah Combs, dancing slow like slowness is what he wants. Seamus is leaning against the far wall with his hands in his pockets, smiling down at the blonde who hogs the mirror in the Ladies.

"Cut in on Da."

"What?" he says.

"Cut in on Da."

"What would I do that for?" he says.

"And you're supposed to be the one with all the brains," I say. "Gobshite."

I walk across the floor and tap Sarah Combs on the back. I tap a rib. She turns, her wide patent belt gleaming in the light that is spilling from the globe above our heads.

"Excuse me," I say, like I'm going to ask her the time.

"Tee-hee," she says, looking down at me. Her eyeballs are cracked like the teapot on our dresser.

"I want to dance with Daddy."

At the word "Daddy" her face changes and she loosens her grip on my father. I take over. The man on the stage is blowing his trumpet now. My father holds my hand tight, like a punishment. I can see my mother on the bench, reaching into her bag for a hanky. Then she goes to the Ladies. There's a feeling like hatred all around Da. I get the feeling he's helpless, but I don't care. For the first time in my life I have some power. I can butt in and take over, rescue and be rescued.

There's a general hullabaloo towards midnight. Everybody's out on the floor, knees buckling, handbags swinging. The Nerves Moran counts down the seconds to the New Year and then there's kissing and hugging. Strange men squeeze me, kiss me like they're thirsty and I'm water.

My parents do not kiss. In all my life, back as far as I remember, I have never seen them touch. Once I took a friend upstairs to show her the house.

"This is Mammy's room, and this is Daddy's room," I said.

"Your parents don't sleep in the same bed?" she said in a voice of pure amazement. And that was when I suspected that our family wasn't normal.

The band picks up the pace. Oh hokey, hokey, pokey!

"Work off them turkey dinners, shake off them plum puddings!" shouts The Nerves Moran and even the ballroom show-offs give up on their figures of eight and do the twist and jive around, and I shimmy around and knock my backside against the mart fella's backside and wind up swinging with a stranger.

Everybody stands for the national anthem. Da is wiping his forehead with a handkerchief and Seamus is panting because he's not used to the exercise. The lights come up and nothing is the same. People are red-faced and sweaty; everything's back to normal. The auctioneer takes over the microphone and thanks a whole lot of different people, and then they auction off a Charolais calf and a goat and batches of tea and sugar and buns and jam, plum puddings and mince pies. There's pebbles where the goat stood and I wonder who'll clean it up. Not until the very last does the raffle take place. The auctioneer holds out the cardboard box of stubs to the blonde.

"Dig deep," he says. "No peeping. First prize a bottle of whiskey."

She takes her time, lapping up the attention.

"Come on," he says, "good girl, it's not the sweepstakes."

She hands him the ticket.

"It's a—What colour is that would ya say, Jimmy? It's a salmon-coloured ticket, number seven hundred and twenty-five. Seven two five. Serial number 3X429H. I'll give ye that again."

It's not mine, but I'm close. I don't want the whiskey anyhow; it'd be kept for the pet lambs. I'd rather the box of Afternoon Tea biscuits that's coming up next. There's a general shuffle, a search in handbags, arse pockets. The auctioneer calls out the numbers a few times and it looks like he'll have to draw again when Mammy rises from her seat. Head held high, she walks in a straight line across the floor. A space opens in the crowd; people step aside to let her pass. Her new high-heeled shoes say *clippety-clippety* on the slippy floor and her red skirt is flaring. I have never seen her do this. Usually she's too shy, gives me the tickets, and I run up and collect the prize.

"Do ya like a drop of the booze, do ya, missus?" The Nerves Moran asks, reading her ticket. "Sure wouldn't it keep ya warm on a night like tonight. No woman needs a man if she has a drop of Power's. Isn't that right? Seven twenty-five, that's the one."

My mother is standing there in her elegant clothes and it's all wrong. She doesn't belong up there.

"Let's check the serial numbers now," he says, drawing it out. "I'm sorry, missus, wrong serial number. The hubby may keep you warm again tonight. Back to the old reliable."

My mother turns and walks *clippety-clippety* back down the slippy floor, with everybody knowing she thought she'd won when she didn't win. And suddenly she is no longer walking, but running, running down in the bright white light, past the cloakroom, towards the door, her hair flailing out like a horse's tail behind her.

Out in the car park snow has accumulated on the trampled grass, the evergreen shelter beds, but the tarmac is wet and shiny in the headlights of cars leaving. Thick, unwavering moonlight shines steadily down on the earth. Ma, Seamus and me sit into the car, shivering, waiting for Da. We can't turn on the engine to heat the car because Da has the keys. My feet are cold as stones. A cloud of greasy steam rises from the open hatch of the chip van, a fat brown sausage painted on the chrome. All around us people are leaving, waving, calling out "Good night!" and "Happy New Year!" They're collecting their chips and driving off.

The chip van has closed its hatch and the car park is empty when Da comes out. He gets into the driver's seat, the ignition catches, a splutter and then we're off, climbing the hill outside the village, winding around the narrow roads towards home.

"That wasn't a bad band," Da says.

Mammy says nothing.

"I said, there was a bit of life in that band." Louder this time.

Still Mammy says nothing.

My father begins to sing "Far Away in Australia." He always sings when he's angry, lets on he's in a good humour when he's raging. The lights of the town are behind us now. These roads are dark. We pass houses with lighted candles in the windows, bulbs blinking on Christmas trees, sheets of newspaper held down on the windscreens of parked cars. Da stops singing before the end of the song.

"Did you see aer a nice little thing in the hall, Seamus?"

"Nothing I'd be mad about."

"That blonde was a nice bit of stuff."

I think about the mart, all the men at the rails bidding for heifers and ewes. I think about Sarah Combs and how she always smells of grassy perfume when we go to her house.

The chestnut tree's boughs at the end of our lane are caked with snow. Da stops the car and we roll back a bit until he puts his foot on the brake. He is waiting for Mammy to get out and open the gates.

Mammy doesn't move.

"Have you got a pain?" he says to her.

She looks straight ahead.

"Is that door stuck or what?" he says.

"Open it yourself."

He reaches across her and opens her door, but she slams it shut.

"Get out there and open that gate!" he barks at me.

Something tells me I should not move.

"Seamus!" he shouts. "Seamus!"

There's not a budge out of any of us.

"By Jeeesus!" he says.

I am afraid. Outside, one corner of my THIS WAY SANTA sign has come loose; the soggy cardboard flaps in the wind. Da turns to my mother, his voice filled with venom.

"And you walking up in your finery in front of all the neighbours, thinking you won first prize in the raffle." He laughs and opens his door. "Running like a tinker out of the hall."

He gets out and there's rage in his walk, as if he's walking on hot coals. He sings: "Far Away in Australia!" He is reaching up, taking the wire off the gate, when a gust of wind blows his hat off. The gates swing open. He stoops to retrieve his hat, but the wind nudges it farther from his reach. He takes another few steps and stoops again to retrieve it, but again it is blown just out of his reach. I think of Santa Claus using the same wrapping paper as us, and suddenly I understand. There is only one obvious explanation.

My father is getting smaller. It feels as if the trees are moving, the chestnut tree whose green hands shelter us in summer is backing away. Then I realise it's the car. We are rolling, sliding backwards. No hand brake and I am not out there putting the stone behind the wheel. And that is when Mammy gets behind the wheel. She slides over into my father's seat, the driver's seat, and puts her foot on the brake. We stop going backwards. She revs up the engine and puts the car in gear. The gear-box grinds—she hasn't the clutch in far enough—but then there's a splutter and we're moving. Mammy is taking us forward, past the Santa sign, past my father, who has stopped singing, through the open gates. She drives us through the snow-covered woods. I can smell the pines. When I look back, my father is standing there watching our taillights. The snow is falling on him, on his bare head, on the hat that he is holding in his hands.

The Tommy Crans

ELIZABETH BOWEN

HERBERT'S FEET, FROM DANGLING SO long in the tram, had died of cold in his boots; he stamped the couple of coffins on blue-and-buff mosaic. In the Tommy Crans' cloakroom the pegs were too high—Uncle Archer cocked H.M.S. *Terrible* for him over a checked ulster. Tommy Cran—aslant meanwhile in the doorway—was an enormous presence. "Come on, now, come!" he exclaimed, and roared with impatience. You would have said he was also arriving at the Tommy Crans' Christmas party, of which one could not bear to miss a moment.

Now into the hall Mrs. Tommy Cran came swimming from elsewhere, dividing with curved little strokes the festive air—hyacinths and gunpowder. Her sleeves, in a thousand ruffles, fled from her elbows. She gained Uncle Archer's lapels and, bobbing, floated from this attachment. Uncle Archer, verifying the mistletoe, loudly kissed her face of delicate pink sugar. "Ha!" yelled Tommy, drawing an unseen dagger. Herbert laughed with embarrassment.

"Only think, Nancy let off all the crackers before tea! She's quite wild, but there are more behind the piano. Ah, is this little Herbert? Herbert …"

"Very well, thank you," said Herbert, and shook hands defensively. This was his first Christmas Day without any father; the news went before him. He had seen his mother off, very brave with the holly wreath, in the cemetery tram. She and father were spending Christmas afternoon together.

Mrs. Tommy Cran stooped to him, bright with a tear-glitter, then with a strong upward sweep, like an angel's, bore him to gaiety. "*Fancy* Nancy!" He fancied Nancy. So by now they would all be wearing the paper caps. Flinging back a white door, she raced Herbert elsewhere.

The room where they all sat seemed to be made of glass, it collected the whole daylight; the candles were still waiting. Over the garden, day still hung like a pink flag; over the trees like frozen feathers, the enchanted icy lake, the lawn. The table was in the window. As Herbert was brought in a clock struck four; the laughing heads all turned in a silence brief as a breath's intake. The great many gentlemen and the rejoicing ladies leaned apart; he and Nancy looked at each other gravely.

He saw Nancy, crowned and serious because she was a queen. Advanced by some urgent pushing, he made his way round the table and sat down beside her, podgily.

She said: "How d'you do? Did you see our lake? It is all frozen. Did you ever see our lake before?"

"I never came here."

"Did you see our two swans?"

She was so beautiful, rolling her ringlets, round with light, on her lacy shoulders, that he said rather shortly: "I shouldn't have thought your lake was large enough for two swans."

"It is, indeed," said Nancy, "it goes round the island. It's large enough for a boat."

They were waiting, around the Christmas cake, for tea to be brought in. Mrs. Tommy Cran shook out the ribbons of her guitar and began to sing again. Very quietly, for a secret, he and Nancy crept to the window; she showed how the lake wound; he could guess how, in summer, her boat would go pushing among the lily leaves. She showed him their boathouse, rusty-red from a lamp inside, solid. "We had a lamp put there for the poor cold swans." (And the swans were asleep beside it.) "How old are you, Herbert?"

"Eight."

"Oh, I'm nine. Do you play brigands?"

"I could," said Herbert.

"Oh, I don't; I'd hate to. But I know some boys who do. Did you have many presents? Uncle Ponto brought me a train; it's more suitable for a boy, really. I could give it to you, perhaps."

"How many uncles—?" began Herbert.

"Ten pretence and none really. I'm adopted, because mummy and daddy have no children. I think that's better fun, don't you?"

"Yes," replied Herbert, after consideration, "anybody could be born."

All the time, Nancy had not ceased to look at him seriously and impersonally. They were both tired already by this afternoon of boisterous grown-up society; they would have liked to be quiet, and though she was loved by ten magic uncles and wore a pearl locket, and he was fat, with spectacles, and felt deformed a little from everybody's knowing about his father, they felt at ease in each other's company.

"Nancy, cut the cake!" exclaimed Mrs. Tommy, and they all clapped their hands for Nancy's attention. So the coloured candles were lit, the garden went dark with loneliness and was immediately curtained out. Two of the uncles put rugs on and bounded about the room like bears and lions; the other faces drew out a crimson brand round the silver teapot. Mrs. Tommy could not bear to put down the guitar, so the teapot fell into the hands of a fuzzy lady with several husbands who cried "Ah, don't, now!" and had to keep brushing gentlemen's hands from her waist. And all the others leaned on one another's shoulders and laughed with gladness because they had been asked to the Tommy Crans'; a dozen times everyone died of laughter and rose again, redder ghosts. Teacups whizzed down a chain of hands. Now Nancy, standing up very straight to cut the cake, was like a doll stitched upright into its box, apt, if you should cut the string at the back, to pitch right forward and break its delicate fingers.

"Oh dear," she sighed, as the knife skidded over the icing. But nobody heard but Herbert. For someone, seeing her white frock over that palace of cake, proposed "The health of the bride."

And an Uncle Joseph, tipping the tea about in his cup, stared and stared with juicy eyes. But nobody saw but Herbert.

"After tea," she whispered, "we'll go and stand on the lake." And after tea they did, while the others played hide-and-seek. Herbert, once looking back through a window, saw uncles chasing the laughing aunts. It was not cold on the lake. Nancy said: "I never believed in fairies—did you either?" She told him she had been given a white muff and was going to be an organist, with an organ of her own. She was going up to Belfast next month to dance for charity. She said she would not give him the train after all; she would give him something really her own, a pink glass greyhound that was an ornament.

When Uncle Archer and Herbert left to walk to the tram terminus, the party was at its brightest. They were singing "Hark the herald" around the drawing-room piano: Nancy sat on her Uncle Joseph's knee, more than politely.

Uncle Archer did not want to go home either. "That was a nice little girl," he said. "Eh?"

Herbert nodded. His uncle, glad that the little chap hadn't had, after all, such a dismal Christmas, pursued heartily: "Kiss her?" Herbert looked quite blank. To tell the truth, this had never occurred to him.

He kissed Nancy later; his death, even, was indirectly caused by his loss of her; but their interchanges were never passionate, and he never knew her better than when they had been standing out on the lake, beyond the cheerful windows. Herbert's mother did not know Uncle Archer's merry friends: she had always loved to live quietly, and, as her need for comfort decreased, she and Herbert saw less, or at least as little as ever of Uncle Archer. So that for years Herbert was not taken again across Dublin to the house with the lake. Once he saw Nancy carry her white muff into a shop, but he stood rooted and did not run after her. Once he saw Mrs. Tommy Cran out in Stephen's Green throwing lollipops to the ducks: but he did not approach; there was nothing to say. He was sent to school, where he painfully learnt to be natural with boys; his sight got no better; they said he must wear glasses all his life. Years later, however, when Herbert was thirteen, the Crans gave a dancing party and did not forget him. He danced once with Nancy; she was silenter now, but she said: "Why did you never come back again?" He could not explain; he trod on her toes and danced heavily on. A Chinese lantern blazed up, and in the confusion he lost her. That evening he saw Mrs. Tommy in tears in the conservatory. Nancy clung, pressing her head, with its drooping pink ribbons, to Mrs. Cran's shoulder; pressing, perhaps, the shoulder against the head. Soon it was all right again and Mrs. Tommy led off in "Sir Roger," but Nancy was like a ghost who presently vanished. A week afterwards he had a letter:

Please meet me to tea at Mitchell's; I want your advice specially.

She was distracted: she had come in to Dublin to sell her gold wristwatch. The Tommy Crans had lost all their money—it wasn't fair to expect them to keep it; they were generous and gay. Nancy had to think hard what must they all do. Herbert went round with her from jeweller to jeweller: these all laughed and paid her nothing but compliments. Her face, with those delicate lovely eyebrows, grew tragic under the fur cap; it rained continuously; she and Herbert looked with incredulity into the grown-up faces: they wondered how one could penetrate far into life without despair. At last a man on the quays gave her eight-and-six for the watch. Herbert, meanwhile, had spent eight shillings of his pocket money on their cab—and, even so, her darling feet were sodden. They were surprised to see, from the window, Tommy Cran jump from an outside car and run joyfully into the Shelbourne. It turned out he had raised some more money from somewhere—as he deserved.

So he sold the house with the lake and moved to an ornamental castle by Dublin Bay. In spite of the grey scene, the transitory light from the sea, the terrace here was gay with urns of geraniums, magnificent with a descent of steps—scrolls and whorls of balustrade, all the grandeur of stucco. Here the band played for their afternoon parties, and here, when they were twenty and twenty-one, Herbert asked Nancy to marry him.

A pug harnessed with bells ran jingling about the terrace. "Oh, I don't know, Herbert; I don't know."

"Do you think you don't love me?"

"I don't know whom I love. Everything would have to be different. Herbert, I don't see how we are ever to live; we seem to know everything. Surely there should be something for us we don't know?" She shut her eyes; they kissed seriously and searchingly. In his arms her body felt soft and voluminous; he could not touch her because of a great fur coat. The coat had been a surprise from Tommy Cran, who loved to give presents on delightful occasions—for now they were off to the Riviera. They were sailing in four days; Nancy and Mrs. Tommy had still all their shopping to do, all his money to spend—he loved them both to be elegant. There was that last party to give before leaving home. Mrs. Tommy could hardly leave the telephone; crossing London, they were to give yet another party, at the Euston Hotel.

"And how could I leave them?" she asked. "They're my business."

"Because they are not quite your parents?"

"Oh, no," she said, eyes reproachful for the misunderstanding he had put up, she knew, only from bitterness. "They would be my affair whoever I was. Don't you see, they're like that."

The Tommy Crans returned from the Riviera subdued, and gave no more parties than they could avoid. They hung sun-yellow curtains, in imitation of the Midi, in all the castle windows, and fortified themselves against despair. They warned their friends they were ruined; they honestly were—and there were heartfelt evenings of consolation. After such evenings, Mrs. Tommy, awaking heavily, whimpered in Nancy's arms, and Tommy approached silence. They had the highest opinion of Nancy, and were restored by her confidence. She knew they would be all right; she assured them they were the best, the happiest people; they were popular—look how Life came back again and again to beg their pardon. And just to show them, she accepted Jeremy Neath and his thousands. So the world could see she was lucky; the world saw the Tommy Crans and their daughter had all the luck. To Herbert she explained nothing. She expected everything of him, on behalf of the Tommy Crans.

The two Crans were distracted by her apotheosis from the incident of their ruin. They had seen her queen of a perpetual Christmas party for six months before they themselves came down magnificently, like an empire. Then Nancy came to fetch them over to England, where her husband had found a small appointment for Tommy, excuse for a pension. But Tommy would not want that long; he had a scheme already, a stunner, a certainty; you just wrote to a hundred people and put in half a crown. That last night he ran about with the leaflets, up and down the uncarpeted castle stairs that were his no longer. He offered to let Herbert in on it; he would yet see Herbert a rich man.

Herbert and Nancy walked after dark on the terrace: she looked ill, tired; she was going to have a baby.

"When I asked you to marry me," he said, "you never answered. You've never answered yet."

She said: "There was no answer. We could never have loved each other and we shall always love each other. We are related."

Herbert, a heavy un-young young man, walked, past desperation, beside her. He did not want peace, but a sword. He returned again and again to the unique moment of her strangeness to him before, as a child, she had spoken. Before, bewildered by all the laughter, he had realised she also was silent.

"You never played games," he said, "or believed in fairies, or anything. I'd have played any game your way; I'd have been good at them. You let them pull all the crackers before tea: now I'd have loved those crackers. That day we met at Mitchell's to sell your watch, you wouldn't have sugar cakes, though I wanted to comfort you. You never asked me out to go round the island in your boat; I'd have died to do that. I never even saw your swans awake. You hold back everything from me and expect me to understand. Why should I understand? In the name of God, what game are we playing?"

"But you do understand?"

"Oh, God," he cried in revulsion. "I don't want to! And now you're going to have a stranger child."

Her sad voice in the dark said: "You said then, 'Anybody could be born!' Herbert, you and I have nothing to do with children—this must be a child like them."

As they turned back to face the window, her smile and voice were tender, but not for him. In the brightly lit stripped room the Tommy Crans walked about together, like lovers in their freedom from each other. They talked of the fortune to be made, the child to be born. Tommy flung his chest out and moved his arms freely in air he did not possess; here and there, pink leaflets fluttered into the dark. The Tommy Crans would go on forever and be continued; their seed should never fail.

Another Christmas

WILLIAM TREVOR

YOU ALWAYS LOOKED BACK, SHE thought. You looked back at other years, other Christmas cards arriving, the children younger. There was the year Patrick had cried, disliking the holly she was decorating the living room with. There was the year Bridget had got a speck of coke in her eye on Christmas Eve and had to be taken to the hospital at Hammersmith in the middle of the night. There was the first year of their marriage, when she and Dermot were still in Waterford. And ever since they'd come to London there was the presence on Christmas Day of their landlord, Mr. Joyce, a man whom they had watched becoming elderly.

She was middle-aged now, with touches of grey in her curly dark hair, a woman known for her cheerfulness, running a bit to fat. Her husband was the opposite: thin and seeming ascetic, with more than a hint of the priest in him, a good man. "Will we get married, Norah?" he'd said one night in the Tara Ballroom in Waterford, 6 November 1953. The proposal had astonished her: it was his brother Ned, heavy and fresh-faced, a different kettle of fish altogether, whom she'd been expecting to make it.

Patiently he held a chair for her while she strung paper-chains across the room, from one picture-rail to another. He warned her to be careful about attaching anything to the electric light. He still held the chair while she put sprigs of holly behind the pictures. He was cautious by nature and alarmed by little things, particularly anxious in case she fell off chairs. He'd never mount a chair himself, to put up decorations or anything else: he'd be useless at it in his opinion and it was his opinion that mattered. He'd never been able to do a thing about the house, but it didn't matter because since the boys had grown up they'd attended to whatever she couldn't manage herself. You wouldn't dream of remarking on it: he was the way he was, considerate and thoughtful in what he did do, teetotal, clever, full of fondness for herself and for the family they'd reared, full of respect for her also.

"Isn't it remarkable how quick it comes round, Norah?" he said while he held the chair. "Isn't it no time since last year?"

"No time at all."

"Though a lot happened in the year, Norah."

"An awful lot happened."

Two of the pictures she decorated were scenes of Waterford: the quays and a man driving sheep past the Bank of Ireland. Her mother had given them to her, taking them down from the hall of the farmhouse.

There was a picture of the Virgin and Child, and other, smaller pictures. She placed her last sprig of holly, a piece with berries on it, above the Virgin's halo.

"I'll make a cup of tea," she said, descending from the chair and smiling at him.

"A cup of tea'd be great, Norah."

The living room, containing three brown armchairs and a table with upright chairs around it, and a sideboard with a television set on it, was crowded by this furniture and seemed even smaller than it was because of the decorations that had been added. On the mantelpiece, above a built-in gas-fire, Christmas cards were arrayed on either side of an ornate green clock.

The house was in a terrace in Fulham. It had always been too small for the family, but now that Patrick and Brendan no longer lived there things were easier. Patrick had married a girl called Pearl six months ago, almost as soon as his period of training with the Midland Bank had ended. Brendan was training in Liverpool, with a firm of computer manufacturers. The three remaining children were still at school, Bridget at the nearby convent, Cathal and Tom at the Sacred Heart Primary. When Patrick and Brendan had moved out the room they'd always shared had become Bridget's. Until then Bridget had slept in her parents' room and she'd have to return there this Christmas because Brendan would be back for three nights. Patrick and Pearl would just come for Christmas Day. They'd be going to Pearl's people, in Croydon, on Boxing Day—St. Stephen's Day, as Norah and Dermot always called it, in the Irish manner.

"It'll be great, having them all," he said. "A family again, Norah."

"And Pearl."

"She's part of us now, Norah."

"Will you have biscuits with your tea? I have a packet of Nice."

He said he would, thanking her. He was a meter-reader with North Thames Gas, a position he had held for twenty-one years, ever since he'd emigrated. In Waterford he'd worked as a clerk in the Customs, not earning very much and not much caring for the stuffy, smoke-laden office he shared with half a dozen other clerks. He had come to England because Norah had thought it was a good idea, because she'd always wanted to work in a London shop. She'd been given a job in Dickins & Jones, in the household linens department, and he'd been taken on as a meter-reader, cycling from door-to-door, remembering the different houses and where the meters were situated in each, being agreeable to householders: all of it suited him from the start. He devoted time to thought while he rode about, and in particular to religious matters.

In her small kitchen she made the tea and carried it on a tray into the living room. She'd been late this year with the decorations. She always liked to get them up a week in advance because they set the mood, making everyone feel right for Christmas. She'd been busy with stuff for a stall Father Malley had asked her to run for his Christmas Sale. A fashion stall he'd called it, but not quite knowing what he meant she'd just asked people for any old clothes they had, jumble really. Because of the time it had taken she hadn't had a minute to see to the decorations until this afternoon, two days before Christmas Eve. But that, as it turned out, had been all for the best. Bridget and Cathal and Tom had gone up to Putney to the pictures, Dermot didn't work on a Monday afternoon: it was convenient that they'd have an hour or two alone together because there was the matter of Mr. Joyce to bring up. Not that she wanted to bring it up, but it couldn't be just left there.

"The cup that cheers," he said, breaking a biscuit in half. Deliberately she put off raising the subject she had in mind. She watched him nibbling the biscuit and then dropping three heaped spoons of sugar into his tea and stirring it. He loved tea. The first time he'd taken her out, to the Savoy cinema in Waterford, they'd had tea afterwards in the cinema café and they'd talked about the film and about people they knew. He'd come to live in Waterford from the country, from the farm his brother had inherited, quite close to her father's farm. He reckoned he'd settled, he told her that night: Waterford wasn't sensational, but it suited him in a lot of ways. If he hadn't married her he'd still be there, working eight hours a day in the Customs and not caring for it, yet managing to get by because he had his religion to assist him.

"Did we get a card from Father Jack yet?" he inquired, referring to a distant cousin, a priest in Chicago.

"Not yet. But it's always on the late side, Father Jack's. It was February last year."

She sipped her tea, sitting in one of the other brown armchairs, on the other side of the gas-fire. It was pleasant being there alone with him in the decorated room, the green clock ticking on the mantelpiece, the Christmas cards, dusk gathering outside. She smiled and laughed, taking another biscuit while he lit a cigarette. "Isn't this great?" she said. "A bit of peace for ourselves?"

Solemnly he nodded.

"Peace comes dropping slow," he said, and she knew he was quoting from some book or other. Quite often he said things she didn't understand. "Peace and goodwill," he added, and she understood that all right.

He tapped the ash from his cigarette into an ashtray which was kept for his use, beside the gas-fire. All his movements were slow. He was a slow thinker, even though he was clever. He arrived at a conclusion, having thought long and carefully; he balanced everything in his mind. "We must think about that, Norah," he said that day, twenty-two years ago, when she'd suggested that they should move to England. A week later he'd said that if she really wanted to he'd agree.

They talked about Bridget and Cathal and Tom. When they came in from the cinema they'd only just have time to change their clothes before setting out again for the Christmas party at Bridget's convent.

"It's a big day for them. Let them lie in in the morning, Norah."

"They could lie in for ever," she said, laughing in case there might seem to be harshness in this recommendation. With Christmas excitement running high, the less she heard from them the better.

"Did you get Cathal the gadgets he wanted?"

"Chemistry stuff. A set in a box."

"You're great the way you manage, Norah."

She denied that. She poured more tea for both of them. She said, as casually as she could:

"Mr. Joyce won't come. I'm not counting him in for Christmas Day."

"He hasn't failed us yet, Norah."

"He won't come this year." She smiled through the gloom at him. "I think we'd best warn the children about it."

"Where would he go if he didn't come here? Where'd he get his dinner?"

"Lyons used to be open in the old days."

"He'd never do that."

"The Bulrush Café has a turkey dinner advertised. There's a lot of people go in for that now. If you have a mother doing a job she maybe hasn't the time for the cooking. They go out to a hotel or a café, three or four pounds a head—"

"Mr. Joyce wouldn't go to a café. No one could go into a café on their own on Christmas Day."

"He won't come here, dear."

It had to be said: it was no good just pretending, laying a place for the old man on an assumption that had no basis to it. Mr. Joyce would not come because Mr. Joyce, last August, had ceased to visit them. Every Friday night he used to come, for a cup of tea and a chat, to watch the nine o'clock news with them. Every Christmas Day he'd brought carefully chosen presents for the children, and chocolates and nuts and cigarettes. He'd given Patrick and Pearl a radio as a wedding present.

"I think he'll come all right. I think maybe he hasn't been too well. God help him, it's a great age, Norah."

"He hasn't been ill, Dermot."

Every Friday Mr. Joyce had sat there in the third of the brown armchairs, watching the television, his bald head inclined so that his good ear was closer to the screen. He was tallish, rather bent now, frail and bony, with a modest white moustache. In his time he'd been a builder; which was how he had come to own property in Fulham, a self-made man who'd never married. That evening in August he had been quite as usual. Bridget had kissed him good night because for as long as she could remember she'd always done that when he came on Friday evenings. He'd asked Cathal how he was getting on with his afternoon paper round.

There had never been any difficulties over the house. They considered that he was fair in his dealings with them; they were his tenants and his friends. When it seemed that the Irish had bombed English people to death in Birmingham and Guildford he did not cease to arrive every Friday evening and on Christmas Day. The bombings were discussed after the news, the Tower of London bomb, the bomb in the bus, and all the others. "Maniacs," Mr. Joyce said and nobody contradicted him.

"He would never forget the children, Norah. Not at Christmastime."

His voice addressed her from the shadows. She felt the warmth of the gas-fire reflected in her face and knew if she looked in a mirror she'd see that she was quite flushed. Dermot's face never reddened. Even though he was nervy, he never displayed emotion. On all occasions his face retained its paleness, his eyes acquired no glimmer of passion. No wife could have a better husband, yet in the matter of Mr. Joyce he was so wrong it almost frightened her.

"Is it tomorrow I call in for the turkey?" he said.

She nodded, hoping he'd ask her if anything was the matter because as a rule she never just nodded in reply to a question. But he didn't say anything. He stubbed his cigarette out. He asked if there was another cup of tea in the pot.

"Dermot, would you take something round to Mr. Joyce?"

"A message, is it?"

"I have a tartan tie for him."

"Wouldn't you give it to him on the day, Norah? Like you always do." He spoke softly, still insisting. She shook her head.

It was all her fault. If she hadn't said they should go to England, if she hadn't wanted to work in a London shop, they wouldn't be caught in the trap they'd made for themselves. Their children spoke with London accents. Patrick and Brendan worked for English firms and would make their homes in England.

Patrick had married an English girl. They were Catholics and they had Irish names, yet home for them was not Waterford.

"Could you make it up with Mr. Joyce, Dermot? Could you go round with the tie and say you were sorry?"

"Sorry?"

"You know what I mean." In spite of herself her voice had acquired a trace of impatience, an edginess that was unusual in it. She did not ever speak to him like that. It was the way she occasionally spoke to the children.

"What would I say I was sorry for, Norah?"

"For what you said that night." She smiled, calming her agitation. He lit another cigarette, the flame of the match briefly illuminating his face. Nothing had changed in his face. He said:

"I don't think Mr. Joyce and I had any disagreement, Norah."

"I know, Dermot. You didn't mean anything—"

"There was no disagreement, girl."

There had been no disagreement, but on that evening in August something else had happened. On the nine o'clock news there had been a report of another outrage and afterwards, when Dermot had turned the television off, there'd been the familiar comment on it. He couldn't understand the mentality of people like that, Mr. Joyce said yet again, killing just anyone, destroying life for no reason. Dermot had shaken his head over it, she herself had said it was uncivilized. Then Dermot had added that they mustn't of course forget what the Catholics in the North had suffered. The bombs were a crime but it didn't do to forget that the crime would not be there if generations of Catholics in the North had not been treated as animals. There'd been a silence then, a difficult kind of silence which she'd broken herself. All that was in the past, she'd said hastily, in a rush, nothing in the past or the present or anywhere else could justify the killing of innocent people. Even so, Dermot had added, it didn't do to avoid the truth. Mr. Joyce had not said anything.

"I'd say there was no need to go round with the tie, Norah. I'd say he'd make the effort on Christmas Day."

"Of course he won't." Her voice was raised, with more than impatience in it now. But her anger was controlled. "Of course he won't come."

"It's a time for goodwill, Norah. Another Christmas: to remind us."

He spoke slowly, the words prompted by some interpretation of God's voice in answer to a prayer. She recognized that in his deliberate tone.

"It isn't just another Christmas. It's an awful kind of Christmas. It's a Christmas to be ashamed, and you're making it worse, Dermot." Her lips were trembling in a way that was uncomfortable. If she tried to calm herself she'd become jittery instead, she might even begin to cry. Mr. Joyce had been generous and tactful, she said loudly. It made no difference to Mr. Joyce that they were Irish people, that their children went to school with the children of I.R.A. men. Yet his generosity and his tact had been thrown back in his face. Everyone knew that the Catholics in the North had suffered, that generations of injustice had been twisted into the shape of a cause. But you couldn't say it to an old man who had hardly been outside Fulham in his life. You couldn't say it because when you did it sounded like an excuse for murder.

"You have to state the truth, Norah. It's there to be told."

"I never yet cared for a North of Ireland person, Catholic or Protestant. Let them fight it out and not bother us."

"You shouldn't say that, Norah."

"It's more of your truth for you."

He didn't reply. There was the gleam of his face for a moment as he drew on his cigarette. In all their married life they had never had a quarrel that was in any way serious, yet she felt herself now in the presence of a seriousness that was too much for her. She had told him that whenever a new bombing took place she prayed it might be the work of the Angry Brigade, or any group that wasn't Irish. She'd told him that in shops she'd begun to feel embarrassed because of her Waterford accent. He'd said she must have courage, and she realized now that he had drawn on courage himself when he'd made the remark to Mr. Joyce. He would have prayed and considered before making it. He would have seen it in the end as his Catholic duty.

"He thinks you don't condemn people being killed." She spoke quietly even though she felt a wildness inside her. She felt she should be out on the streets, shouting in her Waterford accent, violently stating that the bombers were more despicable with every breath they drew, that hatred and death were all they deserved. She saw herself on Fulham Broadway, haranguing the passersby, her greying hair blown in the wind, her voice more passionate than it had ever been before. But none of it was the kind of thing she could do because she was not that kind of woman. She hadn't the courage, any more than she had the courage to urge her anger to explode in their living room. For all the years of her marriage there had never been the need of such courage before: she was aware of that, but found no consolation in it.

"I think he's maybe seen it by now," he said. "How one thing leads to another."

She felt insulted by the words. She willed herself the strength to shout, to pour out a torrent of fury at him, but the strength did not come. Standing up, she stumbled in the gloom and felt a piece of holly under the sole of her shoe. She turned the light on.

"I'll pray that Mr. Joyce will come," he said.

She looked at him, pale and thin, with his priestly face. For the first time since he had asked her to marry him in the Tara Ballroom she did not love him. He was cleverer than she was, yet he seemed half blind. He was good, yet he seemed hard in his goodness, as though he'd be better without it. Up to the very last moment on Christmas Day there would be the pretence that their landlord might arrive, that God would answer a prayer because His truth had been honoured. She considered it hypocrisy, unable to help herself in that opinion.

He talked but she did not listen. He spoke of keeping faith with their own, of being a Catholic. Crime begot crime, he said, God wanted it to be known that one evil led to another. She continued to look at him while he spoke, pretending to listen but wondering instead if in twelve months' time, when another Christmas came, he would still be cycling from house to house to read gas meters. Or would people have objected, requesting a meter-reader who was not Irish? An objection to a man with an Irish accent was down-to-earth and ordinary. It didn't belong in the same grand category as crime begetting crime or God wanting something to be known, or in the category of truth and conscience. In the present circumstances the objection would be understandable and fair. It seemed even right that it should be made, for it was a man with an Irish accent in whom the worst had been brought out by the troubles that had come, who was guilty of a cruelty no one would have believed him capable of. Their harmless, elderly landlord might die in the course of that same year, a friendship he had valued lost, his last Christmas lonely. Grand though it might seem in one way, all of it was petty.

Once, as a girl, she might have cried, but her contented marriage had caused her to lose that habit. She cleared up the tea things, reflecting that the bombers would be pleased if they could note the victory they'd scored in a living room in Fulham. And on Christmas Day, when a family sat down to a conventional meal, the victory would be greater. There would be crackers and chatter and excitement, the Queen and the Pope would deliver speeches. Dermot would discuss these Christmas messages with Patrick and Brendan, as he'd discussed them in the past with Mr. Joyce. He would be as kind as ever. He would console Bridget and Cathal and Tom by saying that Mr. Joyce hadn't been up to the journey. And whenever she looked at him she would remember the Christmases of the past. She would feel ashamed of him, and of herself.

Christmas Eve

MÁIRE MHAC A TSAOI

Translated by Gabriel Fitzmaurice

With candles of angels the sky is now dappled,
The frost on the wind from the hills has a bite,
Kindle the fire and go to your slumber,
Jesus will lie in this household tonight.

Leave all the doors wide open before her,
The Virgin who'll come with the child on her breast,
Grant that you'll stop here tonight, Holy Mary,
That Jesus a while in this household may rest.

The lights were all lighting in that little hostel,
There were generous servings of victuals and wine,
For merchants of silk, for merchants of woollens,
But Jesus will lie in this household tonight.

The Dead

JAMES JOYCE

LILY, THE CARETAKER'S DAUGHTER, WAS literally run off her feet. Hardly had she brought one gentleman into the little pantry behind the office on the ground floor and helped him off with his overcoat than the wheezy hall-door bell clanged again and she had to scamper along the bare hallway to let in another guest. It was well for her she had not to attend to the ladies also. But Miss Kate and Miss Julia had thought of that and had converted the bathroom upstairs into a ladies' dressing room. Miss Kate and Miss Julia were there, gossiping and laughing and fussing, walking after each other to the head of the stairs, peering down over the banisters and calling down to Lily to ask her who had come.

It was always a great affair, the Misses Morkan's annual dance. Everybody who knew them came to it, members of the family, old friends of the family, the members of Julia's choir, any of Kate's pupils that were grown up enough, and even some of Mary Jane's pupils too. Never once had it fallen flat. For years and years it had gone off in splendid style, as long as anyone could remember; ever since Kate and Julia, after the death of their brother Pat, had left the house in Stoney Batter and taken Mary Jane, their only niece, to live with them in the dark, gaunt house on Usher's Island, the upper part of which they had rented from Mr. Fulham, the corn-factor on the ground floor. That was a good thirty years ago if it was a day. Mary Jane, who was then a little girl in short clothes, was now the main prop of the household, for she had the organ in Haddington Road. She had been through the Academy and gave a pupils' concert every year in the upper room of the Antient Concert Rooms. Many of her pupils belonged to the better-class families on the Kingstown and Dalkey line. Old as they were, her aunts also did their share. Julia, though she was quite grey, was still the leading soprano in Adam and Eve's, and Kate, being too feeble to go about much, gave music lessons to beginners on the old square piano in the back room. Lily, the caretaker's daughter, did housemaid's work for them. Though their life was modest, they believed in eating well; the best of everything: diamond-bone sirloins, three-shilling tea and the best bottled stout. But Lily seldom made a mistake in the orders, so that she got on well with her three mistresses. They were fussy, that was all. But the only thing they would not stand was back answers.

Of course, they had good reason to be fussy on such a night. And then it was long after ten o'clock and yet there was no sign of Gabriel and his wife. Besides they were dreadfully afraid that Freddy Malins might turn up screwed. They would not wish for worlds that any of Mary Jane's pupils should see him under the influence; and when he was like that it was sometimes very hard to manage him. Freddy Malins always came late, but they wondered what could be keeping Gabriel: and that was what brought them every two minutes to the banisters to ask Lily had Gabriel or Freddy come.

—O, Mr. Conroy, said Lily to Gabriel when she opened the door for him, Miss Kate and Miss Julia thought you were never coming. Good night, Mrs Conroy.

—I'll engage they did, said Gabriel, but they forget that my wife here takes three mortal hours to dress herself.

He stood on the mat, scraping the snow from his galoshes, while Lily led his wife to the foot of the stairs and called out:

—Miss Kate, here's Mrs. Conroy.

Kate and Julia came toddling down the dark stairs at once. Both of them kissed Gabriel's wife, said she must be perished alive, and asked was Gabriel with her.

—Here I am as right as the mail, Aunt Kate! Go on up. I'll follow, called out Gabriel from the dark.

He continued scraping his feet vigorously while the three women went upstairs, laughing, to the ladies' dressing room. A light fringe of snow lay like a cape on the shoulders of his overcoat and like toe caps on the toes of his goloshes; and, as the buttons of his overcoat slipped with a squeaking noise through the snow-stiffened frieze, a cold, fragrant air from out-of-doors escaped from crevices and folds.

—Is it snowing again, Mr. Conroy? asked Lily.

She had preceded him into the pantry to help him off with his overcoat. Gabriel smiled at the three syllables she had given his surname and glanced at her. She was a slim, growing girl, pale in complexion and with hay-coloured hair. The gas in the pantry made her look still paler. Gabriel had known her when she was a child and used to sit on the lowest step nursing a rag doll.

—Yes, Lily, he answered, and I think we're in for a night of it.

He looked up at the pantry ceiling, which was shaking with the stamping and shuffling of feet on the floor above, listened for a moment to the piano and then glanced at the girl, who was folding his overcoat carefully at the end of a shelf.

—Tell me, Lily, he said in a friendly tone, do you still go to school?

—O no, sir, she answered. I'm done schooling this year and more.

—O, then, said Gabriel gaily, I suppose we'll be going to your wedding one of these fine days with your young man, eh?

The girl glanced back at him over her shoulder and said with great bitterness:

—The men that is now is only all palaver and what they can get out of you.

Gabriel coloured, as if he felt he had made a mistake and, without looking at her, kicked off his goloshes and flicked actively with his muffler at his patent-leather shoes.

He was a stout, tallish young man. The high colour of his cheeks pushed upwards even to his forehead, where it scattered itself in a few formless patches of pale red; and on his hairless face there scintillated restlessly the polished lenses and the bright gilt rims of the glasses which screened his delicate and restless eyes. His glossy black hair was parted in the middle and brushed in a long curve behind his ears where it curled slightly beneath the groove left by his hat.

When he had flicked lustre into his shoes he stood up and pulled his waistcoat down more tightly on his plump body. Then he took a coin rapidly from his pocket.

—O Lily, he said, thrusting it into her hands, it's Christmastime, isn't it? Just … here's a little …

He walked rapidly towards the door.

—O no, sir! cried the girl, following him. Really, sir, I wouldn't take it.

—Christmastime! Christmastime! said Gabriel, almost trotting to the stairs and waving his hand to her in deprecation.

The girl, seeing that he had gained the stairs, called out after him:

—Well, thank you, sir.

He waited outside the drawing room door until the waltz should finish, listening to the skirts that swept against it and to the shuffling of feet. He was still discomposed by the girl's bitter and sudden retort. It had cast a gloom over him which he tried to dispel by arranging his cuffs and the bows of his tie. He then took from his waistcoat pocket a little paper and glanced at the headings he had made for his speech. He was undecided about the lines from Robert Browning, for he feared they would be above the heads of his hearers. Some quotation that they would recognise from Shakespeare or from the Melodies would be better. The indelicate clacking of the men's heels and the shuffling of their soles reminded him that their grade of culture differed from his. He would only make himself ridiculous by quoting poetry to them which they could not understand. They would think that he was airing his superior education. He would fail with them just as he had failed with the girl in the pantry. He had taken up a wrong tone. His whole speech was a mistake from first to last, an utter failure.

Just then his aunts and his wife came out of the ladies' dressing room. His aunts were two small, plainly dressed old women. Aunt Julia was an inch or so the taller. Her hair, drawn low over the tops of her ears, was grey; and grey also, with darker shadows, was her large, flaccid face. Though she was stout in build and stood erect, her slow eyes and parted lips gave her the appearance of a woman who did not know where she was or where she was going. Aunt Kate was more vivacious. Her face, healthier than her sister's, was all puckers and creases, like a shrivelled red apple, and her hair, braided in the same old-fashioned way, had not lost its ripe nut colour.

They both kissed Gabriel frankly. He was their favourite nephew, the son of their dead elder sister, Ellen, who had married T. J. Conroy of the Port and Docks.

—Gretta tells me you're not going to take a cab back to Monkstown tonight, Gabriel, said Aunt Kate.

—No, said Gabriel, turning to his wife, we had quite enough of that last year, hadn't we? Don't you remember, Aunt Kate, what a cold Gretta got out of it? Cab windows rattling all the way, and the east wind blowing in after we passed Merrion. Very jolly it was. Gretta caught a dreadful cold.

Aunt Kate frowned severely and nodded her head at every word.

—Quite right, Gabriel, quite right, she said. You can't be too careful.

—But as for Gretta there, said Gabriel, she'd walk home in the snow if she were let.

Mrs. Conroy laughed.

—Don't mind him, Aunt Kate, she said. He's really an awful bother, what with green shades for Tom's eyes at night and making him do the dumbbells, and forcing Eva to eat the stirabout. The poor child! And she simply hates the sight of it! ... O, but you'll never guess what he makes me wear now!

She broke out into a peal of laughter and glanced at her husband, whose admiring and happy eyes had been wandering from her dress to her face and hair. The two aunts laughed heartily, too, for Gabriel's solicitude was a standing joke with them.

—Goloshes! said Mrs. Conroy. That's the latest. Whenever it's wet underfoot I must put on my goloshes. Tonight even, he wanted me to put them on, but I wouldn't. The next thing he'll buy me will be a diving suit.

Gabriel laughed nervously and patted his tie reassuringly, while Aunt Kate nearly doubled herself, so heartily did she enjoy the joke. The smile soon faded from Aunt Julia's face and her mirthless eyes were directed towards her nephew's face. After a pause she asked:

—And what are goloshes, Gabriel?

—Goloshes, Julia! exclaimed her sister. Goodness me, don't you know what goloshes are? You wear them over your ... over your boots, Gretta, isn't it?

—Yes, said Mrs. Conroy. Guttapercha things. We both have a pair now. Gabriel says everyone wears them on the continent.

—O, on the continent, murmured Aunt Julia, nodding her head slowly.

Gabriel knitted his brows and said, as if he were slightly angered:

—It's nothing very wonderful, but Gretta thinks it very funny because she says the word reminds her of Christy Minstrels.

—But tell me, Gabriel, said Aunt Kate, with brisk tact. Of course, you've seen about the room. Gretta was saying …

—O, the room is all right, replied Gabriel. I've taken one in the Gresham.

—To be sure, said Aunt Kate, by far the best thing to do. And the children, Gretta, you're not anxious about them?

—O, for one night, said Mrs. Conroy. Besides, Bessie will look after them.

—To be sure, said Aunt Kate again. What a comfort it is to have a girl like that, one you can depend on! There's that Lily, I'm sure I don't know what has come over her lately. She's not the girl she was at all.

Gabriel was about to ask his aunt some questions on this point, but she broke off suddenly to gaze after her sister, who had wandered down the stairs and was craning her neck over the banisters.

—Now, I ask you, she said almost testily, where is Julia going? Julia! Julia! Where are you going?

Julia, who had gone half way down one flight, came back and announced blandly:

—Here's Freddy.

At the same moment a clapping of hands and a final flourish of the pianist told that the waltz had ended. The drawing room door was opened from within and some couples came out. Aunt Kate drew Gabriel aside hurriedly and whispered into his ear:

—Slip down, Gabriel, like a good fellow and see if he's all right, and don't let him up if he's screwed. I'm sure he's screwed. I'm sure he is.

Gabriel went to the stairs and listened over the banisters. He could hear two persons talking in the pantry. Then he recognised Freddy Malins' laugh. He went down the stairs noisily.

—It's such a relief, said Aunt Kate to Mrs. Conroy, that Gabriel is here. I always feel easier in my mind when he's here. . . . Julia, there's Miss Daly and Miss Power will take some refreshment. Thanks for your beautiful waltz, Miss Daly. It made lovely time.

A tall, wizen-faced man, with a stiff grizzled moustache and swarthy skin, who was passing out with his partner, said:

—And may we have some refreshment, too, Miss Morkan?

—Julia, said Aunt Kate summarily, and here's Mr. Browne and Miss Furlong. Take them in, Julia, with Miss Daly and Miss Power.

—I'm the man for the ladies, said Mr. Browne, pursing his lips until his moustache bristled and smiling in all his wrinkles. You know, Miss Morkan, the reason they are so fond of me is—

He did not finish his sentence, but, seeing that Aunt Kate was out of earshot, at once led the three young ladies into the back room. The middle of the room was occupied by two square tables placed end to end, and on these Aunt Julia and the caretaker were straightening and smoothing a large cloth. On the sideboard were arrayed dishes and plates, and glasses and bundles of knives and forks and spoons. The top of the closed square piano served also as a sideboard for viands and sweets. At a smaller sideboard in one corner two young men were standing, drinking hop-bitters.

Mr. Browne led his charges thither and invited them all, in jest, to some ladies' punch, hot, strong and sweet. As they said they never took anything strong, he opened three bottles of lemonade for them. Then he asked one of the young men to move aside, and, taking hold of the decanter, filled out for himself a goodly measure of whisky. The young men eyed him respectfully while he took a trial sip.

—God help me, he said, smiling, it's the doctor's orders.

His wizened face broke into a broader smile, and the three young ladies laughed in musical echo to his pleasantry, swaying their bodies to and fro, with nervous jerks of their shoulders. The boldest said:

—O, now, Mr. Browne, I'm sure the doctor never ordered anything of the kind.

Mr. Browne took another sip of his whisky and said, with sidling mimicry:

—Well, you see, I'm like the famous Mrs. Cassidy, who is reported to have said: *Now, Mary Grimes, if I don't take it, make me take it, for I feel I want it.*

His hot face had leaned forward a little too confidentially and he had assumed a very low Dublin accent so that the young ladies, with one instinct, received his speech in silence. Miss Furlong, who was one of Mary Jane's pupils, asked Miss Daly what was the name of the pretty waltz she had played; and Mr. Browne, seeing that he was ignored, turned promptly to the two young men who were more appreciative.

A red-faced young woman, dressed in pansy, came into the room, excitedly clapping her hands and crying:

—Quadrilles! Quadrilles!

Close on her heels came Aunt Kate, crying:

—Two gentlemen and three ladies, Mary Jane!

—O, here's Mr. Bergin and Mr. Kerrigan, said Mary Jane. Mr. Kerrigan, will you take Miss Power? Miss Furlong, may I get you a partner, Mr. Bergin. O, that'll just do now.

—Three ladies, Mary Jane, said Aunt Kate.

The two young gentlemen asked the ladies if they might have the pleasure, and Mary Jane turned to Miss Daly.

—O, Miss Daly, you're really awfully good, after playing for the last two dances, but really we're so short of ladies to-night.

—I don't mind in the least, Miss Morkan.

—But I've a nice partner for you, Mr. Bartell D'Arcy, the tenor. I'll get him to sing later on. All Dublin is raving about him.

—Lovely voice, lovely voice! said Aunt Kate.

As the piano had twice begun the prelude to the first figure Mary Jane led her recruits quickly from the room. They had hardly gone when Aunt Julia wandered slowly into the room, looking behind her at something.

—What is the matter, Julia? asked Aunt Kate anxiously. Who is it?

Julia, who was carrying in a column of table napkins, turned to her sister and said, simply, as if the question had surprised her:

—It's only Freddy, Kate, and Gabriel with him.

In fact right behind her Gabriel could be seen piloting Freddy Malins across the landing. The latter, a young man of about forty, was of Gabriel's size and build, with very round shoulders. His face was fleshy and pallid, touched with colour only at the thick hanging lobes of his ears and at the wide wings of his nose. He had coarse features, a blunt nose, a convex and receding brow, tumid and protruded lips. His heavy-lidded eyes and the disorder of his scanty hair made him look sleepy. He was laughing heartily in a high key at a story which he had been telling Gabriel on the stairs and at the same time rubbing the knuckles of his left fist backwards and forwards into his left eye.

—Good evening, Freddy, said Aunt Julia.

Freddy Malins bade the Misses Morkan good evening in what seemed an offhand fashion by reason of the habitual catch in his voice and then, seeing that Mr. Browne was grinning at him from the sideboard, crossed the room on rather shaky legs and began to repeat in an undertone the story he had just told to Gabriel.

—He's not so bad, is he? said Aunt Kate to Gabriel.

Gabriel's brows were dark but he raised them quickly and answered:

—O, no, hardly noticeable.

—Now, isn't he a terrible fellow! she said. And his poor mother made him take the pledge on New Year's Eve. But come on, Gabriel, into the drawing room.

Before leaving the room with Gabriel she signalled to Mr. Browne by frowning and shaking her forefinger in warning to and fro. Mr. Browne nodded in answer and, when she had gone, said to Freddy Malins:

—Now, then, Teddy, I'm going to fill you out a good glass of lemonade just to buck you up.

Freddy Malins, who was nearing the climax of his story, waved the offer aside impatiently but Mr. Browne, having first called Freddy Malins' attention to a disarray in his dress, filled out and handed him a full glass of lemonade. Freddy Malins' left hand accepted the glass mechanically, his right hand being engaged in the mechanical readjustment of his dress. Mr. Browne, whose face was once more wrinkling with mirth, poured out for himself a glass of whisky while Freddy Malins exploded, before he had well reached the climax of his story, in a kink of high-pitched bronchitic laughter and, setting down his untasted and overflowing glass, began to rub the knuckles of his left fist backwards and forwards into his left eye, repeating words of his last phrase as well as his fit of laughter would allow him.

GABRIEL COULD NOT LISTEN WHILE Mary Jane was playing her Academy piece, full of runs and difficult passages, to the hushed drawing room. He liked music but the piece she was playing had no melody for him and he doubted whether it had any melody for the other listeners, though they had begged Mary Jane to play something. Four young men, who had come from the refreshment room to stand in the doorway at the sound of the piano, had gone away quietly in couples after a few minutes. The only persons who seemed to follow the music were Mary Jane herself, her hands racing along the keyboard or lifted from it at the pauses like those of a priestess in momentary imprecation, and Aunt Kate standing at her elbow to turn the page.

Gabriel's eyes, irritated by the floor, which glittered with beeswax under the heavy chandelier, wandered to the wall above the piano. A picture of the balcony scene in *Romeo and Juliet* hung there and beside it was a picture of the two murdered princes in the Tower which Aunt Julia had worked in red, blue and brown wools when she was a girl. Probably in the school they had gone to as girls that kind of work had been taught for one year. His mother had worked for him as a birthday present a waistcoat of purple tabinet, with little foxes' heads upon it, lined with brown satin and having round mulberry buttons. It was strange that his mother had had no musical talent though Aunt Kate used to call her the brains carrier of the Morkan family. Both she and Julia had always seemed a little proud of their serious and matronly sister. Her photograph stood before the pier glass. She held an open book on her knees and was pointing out something in it to Constantine who, dressed in a man-o'-war suit, lay at her feet. It was she who had chosen the names of her sons for she was very sensible of the dignity of family life. Thanks to her, Constantine was now senior curate in Balbriggan and, thanks to her, Gabriel himself had taken his degree in the Royal University. A shadow passed over his face as he remembered her sullen opposition to his marriage. Some slighting phrases she had used still rankled in his memory; she had once spoken of Gretta as being country cute and that was not true of Gretta at all. It was Gretta who had nursed her during all her last long illness in their house at Monkstown.

He knew that Mary Jane must be near the end of her piece for she was playing again the opening melody with runs of scales after every bar and while he waited for the end the resentment died down in his heart. The piece ended with a trill of octaves in the treble and a final deep octave in the bass. Great applause greeted Mary Jane as, blushing and rolling up her music nervously, she escaped from the room. The most vigorous clapping came from the four young men in the doorway who had gone away to the refreshment room at the beginning of the piece but had come back when the piano had stopped.

Lancers were arranged. Gabriel found himself partnered with Miss Ivors. She was a frank-mannered, talkative young lady, with a freckled face and prominent brown eyes. She did not wear a low-cut bodice and the large brooch which was fixed in the front of her collar bore on it an Irish device and motto.

When they had taken their places she said abruptly:

—I have a crow to pluck with you.

—With me? said Gabriel.

She nodded her head gravely.

—What is it? asked Gabriel, smiling at her solemn manner.

—Who is G. C.? answered Miss Ivors, turning her eyes upon him.

Gabriel coloured and was about to knit his brows, as if he did not understand, when she said bluntly:

—O, innocent Amy! I have found out that you write for *The Daily Express*. Now, aren't you ashamed of yourself?

—Why should I be ashamed of myself? asked Gabriel, blinking his eyes and trying to smile.

—Well, I'm ashamed of you, said Miss Ivors frankly. To say you'd write for a paper like that. I didn't think you were a West Briton.

A look of perplexity appeared on Gabriel's face. It was true that he wrote a literary column every Wednesday in *The Daily Express*, for which he was paid fifteen shillings. But that did not make him a West Briton surely. The books he received for review were almost more welcome than the paltry cheque. He loved to feel the covers and turn over the pages of newly printed books. Nearly every day when his teaching in the college was ended he used to wander down the quays to the secondhand booksellers, to Hickey's on Bachelor's Walk, to Webb's or Massey's on Aston's Quay, or to O'Clohissey's in the bystreet. He did not know how to meet her charge. He wanted to say that literature was above politics. But they were friends of many years' standing and their careers had been parallel, first at the University and then as teachers: he could not risk a grandiose phrase with her. He continued blinking his eyes and trying to smile and murmured lamely that he saw nothing political in writing reviews of books.

When their turn to cross had come he was still perplexed and inattentive. Miss Ivors promptly took his hand in a warm grasp and said in a soft, friendly tone:

—Of course, I was only joking. Come, we cross now.

When they were together again she spoke of the University question and Gabriel felt more at ease. A friend of hers had shown her his review of Browning's poems. That was how she had found out the secret: but she liked the review immensely. Then she said suddenly:

—O, Mr. Conroy, will you come for an excursion to the Aran Isles this summer? We're going to stay there a whole month. It will be splendid out in the Atlantic. You ought to come. Mr. Clancy is coming, and Mr. Kilkelly and Kathleen Kearney. It would be splendid for Gretta too if she'd come. She's from Connacht, isn't she?

—Her people are, said Gabriel shortly.

—But you will come, won't you? said Miss Ivors, laying her warm hand eagerly on his arm.

—The fact is, said Gabriel, I have just arranged to go—

—Go where? asked Miss Ivors.

—Well, you know, every year I go for a cycling tour with some fellows and so—

—But where? asked Miss Ivors.

—Well, we usually go to France or Belgium or perhaps Germany, said Gabriel awkwardly.

—And why do you go to France and Belgium, said Miss Ivors, instead of visiting your own land?

—Well, said Gabriel, it's partly to keep in touch with the languages and partly for a change.

—And haven't you your own language to keep in touch with—Irish? asked Miss Ivors.

—Well, said Gabriel, if it comes to that, you know, Irish is not my language.

Their neighbours had turned to listen to the cross-examination. Gabriel glanced right and left nervously and tried to keep his good humour under the ordeal which was making a blush invade his forehead.

—And haven't you your own land to visit, continued Miss Ivors, that you know nothing of, your own people, and your own country?

—O, to tell you the truth, retorted Gabriel suddenly, I'm sick of my own country, sick of it!

—Why? asked Miss Ivors.

Gabriel did not answer for his retort had heated him.

—Why? repeated Miss Ivors.

They had to go visiting together and, as he had not answered her, Miss Ivors said warmly:

—Of course, you've no answer.

Gabriel tried to cover his agitation by taking part in the dance with great energy. He avoided her eyes for he had seen a sour expression on her face. But when they met in the long chain he was surprised to feel his hand firmly pressed. She looked at him from under her brows for a moment quizzically until he smiled. Then, just as the chain was about to start again, she stood on tiptoe and whispered into his ear:

—West Briton!

When the lancers were over Gabriel went away to a remote corner of the room where Freddy Malins' mother was sitting. She was a stout, feeble old woman with white hair. Her voice had a catch in it like her son's and she stuttered slightly. She had been told that Freddy had come and that he was nearly all right. Gabriel asked her whether she had had a good crossing. She lived with her married daughter in Glasgow and came to Dublin on a visit once a year. She answered placidly that she had had a beautiful crossing and that the captain had been most attentive to her. She spoke also of the beautiful house her daughter kept in Glasgow, and of all the friends they had there. While her tongue rambled on Gabriel tried to banish from his mind all memory of the unpleasant incident with Miss Ivors. Of course the girl or woman, or whatever she was, was an enthusiast but there was a time for all things. Perhaps he ought not to have answered her like that. But she had no right to call him a West Briton before people, even in joke. She had tried to make him ridiculous before people, heckling him and staring at him with her rabbit's eyes.

He saw his wife making her way towards him through the waltzing couples. When she reached him she said into his ear:

—Gabriel, Aunt Kate wants to know won't you carve the goose as usual. Miss Daly will carve the ham and I'll do the pudding.

—All right, said Gabriel.

—She's sending in the younger ones first as soon as this waltz is over so that we'll have the table to ourselves.

—Were you dancing? asked Gabriel.

—Of course I was. Didn't you see me? What row had you with Molly Ivors?

—No row. Why? Did she say so?

—Something like that. I'm trying to get that Mr. D'Arcy to sing. He's full of conceit, I think.

—There was no row, said Gabriel moodily, only she wanted me to go for a trip to the west of Ireland and I said I wouldn't.

His wife clasped her hands excitedly and gave a little jump.

—O, do go, Gabriel, she cried. I'd love to see Galway again.

—You can go if you like, said Gabriel coldly.

She looked at him for a moment, then turned to Mrs. Malins and said:

—There's a nice husband for you, Mrs. Malins.

While she was threading her way back across the room Mrs. Malins, without adverting to the interruption, went on to tell Gabriel what beautiful places there were in Scotland and beautiful scenery. Her son-in-law brought them every year to the lakes and they used to go fishing. Her son-in-law was a splendid fisher. One day he caught a beautiful big fish and the man in the hotel cooked it for their dinner.

Gabriel hardly heard what she said. Now that supper was coming near he began to think again about his speech and about the quotation. When he saw Freddy Malins coming across the room to visit his mother Gabriel left the chair free for him and retired into the embrasure of the window. The room had already cleared and from the back room came the clatter of plates and knives. Thosc who still remained in the drawing room seemed tired of dancing and were conversing quietly in little groups. Gabriel's warm trembling fingers tapped the cold pane of the window. How cool it must be outside! How pleasant it would be to walk out alone, first along by the river and then through the park! The snow would be lying on the branches of the trees and forming a bright cap on the top of the Wellington Monument. How much more pleasant it would be there than at the supper table!

He ran over the headings of his speech: Irish hospitality, sad memories, the Three Graces, Paris, the quotation from Browning. He repeated to himself a phrase he had written in his review: *One feels that one is listening to a thought-tormented music.* Miss Ivors had praised the review. Was she sincere? Had she really any life of her own behind all her propagandism? There had never been any ill-feeling between them until that night. It unnerved him to think that she would be at the supper table, looking up at him while he spoke with her critical quizzing eyes. Perhaps she would not be sorry to see him fail in his speech. An idea came into his mind and gave him courage. He would say, alluding to Aunt Kate and Aunt Julia: *Ladies and Gentlemen, the generation which is now on the wane among us may have had its faults but for my part I think it had certain qualities of hospitality, of humour, of humanity, which the new and very serious and hypereducated generation that is growing up around us seems to me to lack.* Very good: that was one for Miss Ivors. What did he care that his aunts were only two ignorant old women?

A murmur in the room attracted his attention. Mr. Browne was advancing from the door, gallantly escorting Aunt Julia, who leaned upon his arm, smiling and hanging her head. An irregular musketry of applause escorted her also as far as the piano and then, as Mary Jane seated herself on the stool, and Aunt Julia, no longer smiling, half turned so as to pitch her voice fairly into the room, gradually ceased. Gabriel recognised the prelude. It was that of an old song of Aunt Julia's—"Arrayed for the Bridal." Her voice, strong and clear in tone, attacked with great spirit the runs which embellish the air and though she sang very rapidly she did not miss even the smallest of the grace notes. To follow the voice, without looking at the singer's face, was to feel and share the excitement of swift and secure flight. Gabriel applauded loudly with all the others at the close of the song and loud applause was borne in from the invisible supper table. It sounded so genuine that a little colour struggled into Aunt Julia's face as she bent to replace in the music stand the old, leather-bound songbook that had her initials on the cover. Freddy Malins, who had listened with his head perched sideways to hear her better, was still applauding when everyone else had ceased and talking animatedly to his mother who nodded her head gravely and slowly in acquiescence. At last, when he could clap no more, he stood up suddenly and hurried across the room to Aunt Julia whose hand he seized and held in both his hands, shaking it when words failed him or the catch in his voice proved too much for him.

—I was just telling my mother, he said, I never heard you sing so well, never. No, I never heard your voice so good as it is tonight. Now! Would you believe that now? That's the truth. Upon my word and honour that's the truth. I never heard your voice sound so fresh and so . . . so clear and fresh, never.

Aunt Julia smiled broadly and murmured something about compliments as she released her hand from his grasp. Mr. Browne extended his open hand towards her and said to those who were near him in the manner of a showman introducing a prodigy to an audience:

—Miss Julia Morkan, my latest discovery!

He was laughing very heartily at this himself when Freddy Malins turned to him and said:

—Well, Browne, if you're serious you might make a worse discovery. All I can say is I never heard her sing half so well as long as I am coming here. And that's the honest truth.

—Neither did I, said Mr. Browne. I think her voice has greatly improved.

Aunt Julia shrugged her shoulders and said with meek pride:

—Thirty years ago I hadn't a bad voice as voices go.

—I often told Julia, said Aunt Kate emphatically, that she was simply thrown away in that choir. But she never would be said by me.

She turned as if to appeal to the good sense of the others against a refractory child while Aunt Julia gazed in front of her, a vague smile of reminiscence playing on her face.

—No, continued Aunt Kate, she wouldn't be said or led by anyone, slaving there in that choir night and day, night and day. Six o'clock on Christmas morning! And all for what?

—Well, isn't it for the honour of God, Aunt Kate? asked Mary Jane, twisting round on the piano stool and smiling.

Aunt Kate turned fiercely on her niece and said:

—I know all about the honour of God, Mary Jane, but I think it's not at all honourable for the pope to turn out the women out of the choirs that have slaved there all their lives and put little whippersnappers of boys over their heads. I suppose it is for the good of the Church if the pope does it. But it's not just, Mary Jane, and it's not right.

She had worked herself into a passion and would have continued in defence of her sister for it was a sore subject with her but Mary Jane, seeing that all the dancers had come back, intervened pacifically:

—Now, Aunt Kate, you're giving scandal to Mr. Browne who is of the other persuasion.

Aunt Kate turned to Mr. Browne, who was grinning at this allusion to his religion, and said hastily:

—O, I don't question the pope's being right. I'm only a stupid old woman and I wouldn't presume to do such a thing. But there's such a thing as common everyday politeness and gratitude. And if I were in Julia's place I'd tell that Father Healey straight up to his face …

—And besides, Aunt Kate, said Mary Jane, we really are all hungry and when we are hungry we are all very quarrelsome.

—And when we are thirsty we are also quarrelsome, added Mr. Browne.

—So that we had better go to supper, said Mary Jane, and finish the discussion afterwards.

On the landing outside the drawing room Gabriel found his wife and Mary Jane trying to persuade Miss Ivors to stay for supper. But Miss Ivors, who had put on her hat and was buttoning her cloak, would not stay. She did not feel in the least hungry and she had already overstayed her time.

—But only for ten minutes, Molly, said Mrs. Conroy. That won't delay you.

—To take a pick itself, said Mary Jane, after all your dancing.

—I really couldn't, said Miss Ivors.

—I am afraid you didn't enjoy yourself at all, said Mary Jane hopelessly.

—Ever so much, I assure you, said Miss Ivors, but you really must let me run off now.

—But how can you get home? asked Mrs. Conroy.

—O, it's only two steps up the quay.

Gabriel hesitated a moment and said:

—If you will allow me, Miss Ivors, I'll see you home if you are really obliged to go.

But Miss Ivors broke away from them.

—I won't hear of it, she cried. For goodness' sake go in to your suppers and don't mind me. I'm quite well able to take care of myself.

—Well, you're the comical girl, Molly, said Mrs. Conroy frankly.

—*Beannacht libh*, cried Miss Ivors, with a laugh, as she ran down the staircase.

Mary Jane gazed after her, a moody puzzled expression on her face, while Mrs. Conroy leaned over the banisters to listen for the hall door. Gabriel asked himself was he the cause of her abrupt departure. But she did not seem to be in ill humour: she had gone away laughing. He stared blankly down the staircase.

At the moment Aunt Kate came toddling out of the supper room, almost wringing her hands in despair.

—Where is Gabriel? she cried. Where on earth is Gabriel? There's everyone waiting in there, stage to let, and nobody to carve the goose!

—Here I am, Aunt Kate! cried Gabriel, with sudden animation, ready to carve a flock of geese, if necessary.

A fat brown goose lay at one end of the table and at the other end, on a bed of creased paper strewn with sprigs of parsley, lay a great ham, stripped of its outer skin and peppered over with crust crumbs, a neat paper frill round its shin and beside this was a round of spiced beef. Between these rival ends ran parallel lines of side dishes: two little minsters of jelly, red and yellow; a shallow dish full of blocks of blancmange and red jam; a large green leaf-shaped dish with a stalk-shaped handle, on which lay bunches of purple raisins and peeled almonds; a companion dish on which lay a solid rectangle of Smyrna figs; a dish of custard topped with grated nutmeg; a small bowl full of chocolates and sweets wrapped in gold and silver papers and a glass vase in which stood some tall celery stalks. In the centre of the table there stood, as sentries to a fruit stand which upheld a pyramid of oranges and American apples, two squat, old-fashioned decanters of cut glass, one containing port and the other dark sherry. On the closed square piano a pudding in a huge yellow dish lay in waiting and behind it were three squads of bottles of stout and ale and minerals, drawn up according to the colours of their uniforms, the first two black, with brown-and-red labels, the third and smallest squad white, with transverse green sashes.

Gabriel took his seat boldly at the head of the table and, having looked to the edge of the carver, plunged his fork firmly into the goose. He felt quite at ease now for he was an expert carver and liked nothing better than to find himself at the head of a well-laden table.

—Miss Furlong, what shall I send you? he asked. A wing or a slice of the breast?

—Just a small slice of the breast.

—Miss Higgins, what for you?

—O, anything at all, Mr. Conroy.

While Gabriel and Miss Daly exchanged plates of goose and plates of ham and spiced beef Lily went from guest to guest with a dish of hot floury potatoes wrapped in a white napkin. This was Mary Jane's idea and she had also suggested applesauce for the goose but Aunt Kate had said that plain roast goose without any applesauce had always been good enough for her and she hoped she might never eat worse. Mary Jane waited on her pupils and saw that they got the best slices and Aunt Kate and Aunt Julia opened and carried across from the piano bottles of stout and ale for the gentlemen and bottles of minerals for the ladies. There was a great deal of confusion and laughter and noise, the noise of orders and counter orders, of knives and forks, of corks and glass-stoppers. Gabriel began to carve second helpings as soon as he had finished the first round without serving himself. Everyone protested loudly so that he compromised by taking a long draught of stout for he had found the carving hot work. Mary Jane settled down quietly to her supper but Aunt Kate and Aunt Julia were still toddling round the table, walking on each other's heels, getting in each other's way and giving each other unheeded orders. Mr. Browne begged of them to sit down and eat their suppers and so did Gabriel but they said there was time enough, so that, at last, Freddy Malins stood up and, capturing Aunt Kate, plumped her down on her chair amid general laughter.

When everyone had been well served Gabriel said, smiling:

—Now, if anyone wants a little more of what vulgar people call stuffing let him or her speak.

A chorus of voices invited him to begin his own supper and Lily came forward with three potatoes which she had reserved for him.

—Very well, said Gabriel amiably, as he took another preparatory draught, kindly forget my existence, ladies and gentlemen, for a few minutes.

He set to his supper and took no part in the conversation with which the table covered Lily's removal of the plates. The subject of talk was the opera company which was then at the Theatre Royal. Mr. Bartell D'Arcy, the tenor, a dark-complexioned young man with a smart moustache, praised very highly the leading contralto of the company but Miss Furlong thought she had a rather vulgar style of production. Freddy Malins said there was a Negro chieftain singing in the second part of the Gaiety pantomime who had one of the finest tenor voices he had ever heard.

—Have you heard him? he asked Mr. Bartell D'Arcy across the table.

—No, answered Mr. Bartell D'Arcy carelessly.

—Because, Freddy Malins explained, now I'd be curious to hear your opinion of him. I think he has a grand voice.

—It takes Teddy to find out the really good things, said Mr. Browne familiarly to the table.

—And why couldn't he have a voice too? asked Freddy Malins sharply. Is it because he's only a black?

Nobody answered this question and Mary Jane led the table back to the legitimate opera. One of her pupils had given her a pass for *Mignon*. Of course it was very fine, she said, but it made her think of poor Georgina Burns. Mr. Browne could go back farther still, to the old Italian companies that used to come to Dublin—Tietjens, Ilma de Murzka, Campanini, the great Trebelli Giuglini, Ravelli, Aramburo. Those were the days, he said, when there was something like singing to be heard in Dublin. He told, too, of how the top gallery of the old Royal used to be packed night after night, of how one night an Italian tenor had sung five encores to "Let Me Like a Soldier Fall," introducing a high C every time, and of how the gallery boys would sometimes in their enthusiasm unyoke the horses from the carriage of some great prima donna and pull her themselves through the streets to her hotel. Why did they never play the grand old operas now, he asked, *Dinorah, Lucrezia Borgia*? Because they could not get the voices to sing them: that was why.

—O, well, said Mr. Bartell D'Arcy, I presume there are as good singers to-day as there were then.

—Where are they? asked Mr. Browne defiantly.

—In London, Paris, Milan, said Mr. Bartell D'Arcy warmly. I suppose Caruso, for example, is quite as good, if not better than any of the men you have mentioned.

—Maybe so, said Mr. Browne. But I may tell you I doubt it strongly.

—O, I'd give anything to hear Caruso sing, said Mary Jane.

—For me, said Aunt Kate, who had been picking a bone, there was only one tenor. To please me, I mean. But I suppose none of you ever heard of him.

—Who was he, Miss Morkan? asked Mr. Bartell D'Arcy politely.

—His name, said Aunt Kate, was Parkinson. I heard him when he was in his prime and I think he had then the purest tenor voice that was ever put into a man's throat.

—Strange, said Mr. Bartell D'Arcy. I never even heard of him.

—Yes, yes, Miss Morkan is right, said Mr. Browne. I remember hearing of old Parkinson but he's too far back for me.

—A beautiful, pure, sweet, mellow English tenor, said Aunt Kate with enthusiasm.

Gabriel having finished, the huge pudding was transferred to the table. The clatter of forks and spoons began again. Gabriel's wife served out spoonfuls of the pudding and passed the plates down the table. Midway down they were held up by Mary Jane, who replenished them with raspberry or orange jelly or with blancmange and jam. The pudding was of Aunt Julia's making and she received praises for it from all quarters. She herself said that it was not quite brown enough.

—Well, I hope, Miss Morkan, said Mr. Browne, that I'm brown enough for you because, you know, I'm all brown.

All the gentlemen, except Gabriel, ate some of the pudding out of compliment to Aunt Julia. As Gabriel never ate sweets the celery had been left for him. Freddy Malins also took a stalk of celery and ate it with his pudding. He had been told that celery was a capital thing for the blood and he was just then under doctor's care. Mrs. Malins, who had been silent all through the supper, said that her son was going down to Mount Melleray in a week or so. The table then spoke of Mount Melleray, how bracing the air was down there, how hospitable the monks were and how they never asked for a penny-piece from their guests.

—And do you mean to say, asked Mr. Browne incredulously, that a chap can go down there and put up there as if it were a hotel and live on the fat of the land and then come away without paying anything?

—O, most people give some donation to the monastery when they leave, said Mary Jane.

—I wish we had an institution like that in our Church, said Mr. Browne candidly.

He was astonished to hear that the monks never spoke, got up at two in the morning and slept in their coffins. He asked what they did it for.

—That's the rule of the order, said Aunt Kate firmly.

—Yes, but why? asked Mr. Browne.

Aunt Kate repeated that it was the rule, that was all. Mr. Browne still seemed not to understand. Freddy Malins explained to him, as best he could, that the monks were trying to make up for the sins committed by all the sinners in the outside world. The explanation was not very clear for Mr. Browne grinned and said:

—I like that idea very much but wouldn't a comfortable spring bed do them as well as a coffin?

—The coffin, said Mary Jane, is to remind them of their last end.

As the subject had grown lugubrious it was buried in a silence of the table during which Mrs. Malins could be heard saying to her neighbour in an indistinct undertone:

—They are very good men, the monks, very pious men.

The raisins and almonds and figs and apples and oranges and chocolates and sweets were now passed about the table and Aunt Julia invited all the guests to have either port or sherry. At first Mr. Bartell D'Arcy refused to take either but one of his neighbours nudged him and whispered something to him upon which he allowed his glass to be filled. Gradually as the last glasses were being filled the conversation ceased. A pause followed, broken only by the noise of the wine and by unsettlings of chairs. The Misses Morkan, all three, looked down at the tablecloth. Someone coughed once or twice and then a few gentlemen patted the table gently as a signal for silence. The silence came and Gabriel pushed back his chair and stood up.

The patting at once grew louder in encouragement and then ceased altogether. Gabriel leaned his ten trembling fingers on the tablecloth and smiled nervously at the company. Meeting a row of upturned faces he raised his eyes to the chandelier. The piano was playing a waltz tune and he could hear the skirts sweeping against the drawing room door. People, perhaps, were standing in the snow on the quay outside, gazing up at the lighted windows and listening to the waltz music. The air was pure there. In the distance lay the park where the trees were weighted with snow. The Wellington Monument wore a gleaming cap of snow that flashed westward over the white field of Fifteen Acres.

He began:

—Ladies and Gentlemen,

—It has fallen to my lot this evening, as in years past, to perform a very pleasing task but a task for which I am afraid my poor powers as a speaker are all too inadequate.

—No, no! said Mr. Browne.

—But, however that may be, I can only ask you tonight to take the will for the deed and to lend me your attention for a few moments while I endeavour to express to you in words what my feelings are on this occasion.

—Ladies and Gentlemen, it is not the first time that we have gathered together under this hospitable roof, around this hospitable board. It is not the first time that we have been the recipients—or perhaps, I had better say, the victims—of the hospitality of certain good ladies.

He made a circle in the air with his arm and paused. Everyone laughed or smiled at Aunt Kate and Aunt Julia and Mary Jane who all turned crimson with pleasure. Gabriel went on more boldly:

—I feel more strongly with every recurring year that our country has no tradition which does it so much honour and which it should guard so jealously as that of its hospitality. It is a tradition that is unique as far as my experience goes (and I have visited not a few places abroad) among the modern nations. Some would say, perhaps, that with us it is rather a failing than anything to be boasted of. But granted even that, it is, to my mind, a princely failing, and one that I trust will long be cultivated among us. Of one thing, at least, I am sure. As long as this one roof shelters the good ladies aforesaid—and I wish from my heart it may do so for many and many a long year to come—the tradition of genuine warmhearted courteous Irish hospitality, which our forefathers have handed down to us and which we in turn must hand down to our descendants, is still alive among us.

A hearty murmur of assent ran round the table. It shot through Gabriel's mind that Miss Ivors was not there and that she had gone away discourteously: and he said with confidence in himself:

—Ladies and Gentlemen,

—A new generation is growing up in our midst, a generation actuated by new ideas and new principles. It is serious and enthusiastic for these new ideas and its enthusiasm, even when it is misdirected, is, I believe, in the main sincere. But we are living in a sceptical and, if I may use the phrase, a thought-tormented age: and sometimes I fear that this new generation, educated or hypereducated as it is, will lack those qualities of humanity, of hospitality, of kindly humour which belonged to an older day. Listening tonight to the names of all those great singers of the past it seemed to me, I must confess, that we were living in a less spacious age. Those days might, without exaggeration, be called spacious days: and if they are gone beyond recall let us hope, at least, that in gatherings such as this we shall still speak of them with pride and affection, still cherish in our hearts the memory of those dead and gone great ones whose fame the world will not willingly let die.

—Hear, hear! said Mr. Browne loudly.

—But yet, continued Gabriel, his voice falling into a softer inflection, there are always in gatherings such as this sadder thoughts that will recur to our minds: thoughts of the past, of youth, of changes, of absent faces that we miss here tonight. Our path through life is strewn with many such sad memories: and were we to brood upon them always we could not find the heart to go on bravely with our work among the living. We have all of us living duties and living affections which claim, and rightly claim, our strenuous endeavours.

—Therefore, I will not linger on the past. I will not let any gloomy moralising intrude upon us here tonight. Here we are gathered together for a brief moment from the bustle and rush of our everyday routine. We are met here as friends, in the spirit of good-fellowship, as colleagues, also to a certain extent, in the true spirit of *camaraderie*, and as the guests of—what shall I call them?—the Three Graces of the Dublin musical world.

The table burst into applause and laughter at this allusion. Aunt Julia vainly asked each of her neighbours in turn to tell her what Gabriel had said.

—He says we are the Three Graces, Aunt Julia, said Mary Jane.

Aunt Julia did not understand but she looked up, smiling, at Gabriel, who continued in the same vein:

—Ladies and Gentlemen,

—I will not attempt to play tonight the part that Paris played on another occasion. I will not attempt to choose between them. The task would be an invidious one and one beyond my poor powers. For when I view them in turn, whether it be our chief hostess herself, whose good heart, whose too good heart, has become a byword with all who know her, or her sister, who seems to be gifted with perennial youth and whose singing must have been a surprise and a revelation to us all tonight, or, last but not least, when I consider our youngest hostess, talented, cheerful, hard-working and the best of nieces, I confess, Ladies and Gentlemen, that I do not know to which of them I should award the prize.

Gabriel glanced down at his aunts and, seeing the large smile on Aunt Julia's face and the tears which had risen to Aunt Kate's eyes, hastened to his close. He raised his glass of port gallantly, while every member of the company fingered a glass expectantly, and said loudly:

—Let us toast them all three together. Let us drink to their health, wealth, long life, happiness and prosperity and may they long continue to hold the proud and self-won position which they hold in their profession and the position of honour and affection which they hold in our hearts.

All the guests stood up, glass in hand, and turning towards the three seated ladies, sang in unison, with Mr. Browne as leader:

For they are jolly gay fellows,
For they are jolly gay fellows,
For they are jolly gay fellows,
Which nobody can deny.

Aunt Kate was making frank use of her handkerchief and even Aunt Julia seemed moved. Freddy Malins beat time with his pudding-fork and the singers turned towards one another, as if in melodious conference, while they sang with emphasis:

Unless he tells a lie,
Unless he tells a lie,

Then, turning once more towards their hostesses, they sang:

For they are jolly gay fellows,
For they are jolly gay fellows,
For they are jolly gay fellows,
Which nobody can deny.

The acclamation which followed was taken up beyond the door of the supper room by many of the other guests and renewed time after time, Freddy Malins acting as officer with his fork on high.

THE PIERCING MORNING AIR CAME into the hall where they were standing so that Aunt Kate said:

—Close the door, somebody. Mrs. Malins will get her death of cold.

—Browne is out there, Aunt Kate, said Mary Jane.

—Browne is everywhere, said Aunt Kate, lowering her voice.

Mary Jane laughed at her tone.

—Really, she said archly, he is very attentive.

—He has been laid on here like the gas, said Aunt Kate in the same tone, all during the Christmas.

She laughed herself this time good-humouredly and then added quickly:

—But tell him to come in, Mary Jane, and close the door. I hope to goodness he didn't hear me.

At that moment the hall door was opened and Mr. Browne came in from the doorstep, laughing as if his heart would break. He was dressed in a long green overcoat with mock astrakhan cuffs and collar and wore on his head an oval fur cap. He pointed down the snow-covered quay from where the sound of shrill prolonged whistling was borne in.

—Teddy will have all the cabs in Dublin out, he said.

Gabriel advanced from the little pantry behind the office, struggling into his overcoat and, looking round the hall, said:

—Gretta not down yet?

—She's getting on her things, Gabriel, said Aunt Kate.

—Who's playing up there? asked Gabriel.

—Nobody. They're all gone.

—O no, Aunt Kate, said Mary Jane. Bartell D'Arcy and Miss O'Callaghan aren't gone yet.

—Someone is fooling at the piano anyhow, said Gabriel.

Mary Jane glanced at Gabriel and Mr. Browne and said with a shiver:

—It makes me feel cold to look at you two gentlemen muffled up like that. I wouldn't like to face your journey home at this hour.

—I'd like nothing better this minute, said Mr. Browne stoutly, than a rattling fine walk in the country or a fast drive with a good spanking goer between the shafts.

—We used to have a very good horse and trap at home, said Aunt Julia sadly.

—The never-to-be-forgotten Johnny, said Mary Jane, laughing.

Aunt Kate and Gabriel laughed too.

—Why, what was wonderful about Johnny? asked Mr. Browne.

—The late lamented Patrick Morkan, our grandfather, that is, explained Gabriel, commonly known in his later years as the old gentleman, was a glue-boiler.

—O, now, Gabriel, said Aunt Kate, laughing, he had a starch mill.

—Well, glue or starch, said Gabriel, the old gentleman had a horse by the name of Johnny. And Johnny used to work in the old gentleman's mill, walking round and round in order to drive the mill. That was all very well; but now comes the tragic part about Johnny. One fine day the old gentleman thought he'd like to drive out with the quality to a military review in the park.

—The Lord have mercy on his soul, said Aunt Kate compassionately.

—Amen, said Gabriel. So the old gentleman, as I said, harnessed Johnny and put on his very best tall hat and his very best stock collar and drove out in grand style from his ancestral mansion somewhere near Back Lane, I think.

Everyone laughed, even Mrs. Malins, at Gabriel's manner and Aunt Kate said:

—O, now, Gabriel, he didn't live in Back Lane, really. Only the mill was there.

—Out from the mansion of his forefathers, continued Gabriel, he drove with Johnny. And everything went on beautifully until Johnny came in sight of King Billy's statue: and whether he fell in love with the horse King Billy sits on or whether he thought he was back again in the mill, anyhow he began to walk round the statue.

Gabriel paced in a circle round the hall in his goloshes amid the laughter of the others.

—Round and round he went, said Gabriel, and the old gentleman, who was a very pompous old gentleman, was highly indignant. *Go on, sir! What do you mean, sir? Johnny! Johnny! Most extraordinary conduct! Can't understand the horse!*

The peals of laughter which followed Gabriel's imitation of the incident was interrupted by a resounding knock at the hall door. Mary Jane ran to open it and let in Freddy Malins. Freddy Malins, with his hat well back on his head and his shoulders humped with cold, was puffing and steaming after his exertions.

—I could only get one cab, he said.

—O, we'll find another along the quay, said Gabriel.

—Yes, said Aunt Kate. Better not keep Mrs. Malins standing in the draught.

Mrs. Malins was helped down the front steps by her son and Mr. Browne and, after many manœuvres, hoisted into the cab. Freddy Malins clambered in after her and spent a long time settling her on the seat, Mr. Browne helping him with advice. At last she was settled comfortably and Freddy Malins invited Mr. Browne into the cab. There was a good deal of confused talk, and then Mr. Browne got into the cab. The cabman settled his rug over his knees, and bent down for the address. The confusion grew greater and the cabman was directed differently by Freddy Malins and Mr. Browne, each of whom had his head out through a window of the cab. The difficulty was to know where to drop Mr. Browne along the route, and Aunt Kate, Aunt Julia and Mary Jane helped the discussion from the doorstep with cross-directions and contradictions and abundance of laughter. As for Freddy Malins he was speechless with laughter. He popped his head in and out of the window every moment to the great danger of his hat, and told his mother how the discussion was progressing, till at last Mr. Browne shouted to the bewildered cabman above the din of everybody's laughter:

—Do you know Trinity College?

—Yes, sir, said the cabman.

—Well, drive bang up against Trinity College gates, said Mr. Browne, and then we'll tell you where to go. You understand now?

—Yes, sir, said the cabman.

—Make like a bird for Trinity College.

—Right, sir, said the cabman.

The horse was whipped up and the cab rattled off along the quay amid a chorus of laughter and adieus.

Gabriel had not gone to the door with the others. He was in a dark part of the hall gazing up the staircase. A woman was standing near the top of the first flight, in the shadow also. He could not see her face but he could see the terra-cotta and salmon-pink panels of her skirt which the shadow made appear black and white. It was his wife. She was leaning on the banisters, listening to something. Gabriel was surprised at her stillness and strained his ear to listen also. But he could hear little save the noise of laughter and dispute on the front steps, a few chords struck on the piano and a few notes of a man's voice singing.

He stood still in the gloom of the hall, trying to catch the air that the voice was singing and gazing up at his wife. There was grace and mystery in her attitude as if she were a symbol of something. He asked himself what is a woman standing on the stairs in the shadow, listening to distant music, a symbol of. If he were a painter he would paint her in that attitude. Her blue felt hat would show off the bronze of her hair against the darkness and the dark panels of her skirt would show off the light ones. *Distant Music* he would call the picture if he were a painter.

The hall door was closed; and Aunt Kate, Aunt Julia and Mary Jane came down the hall, still laughing.

—Well, isn't Freddy terrible? said Mary Jane. He's really terrible.

Gabriel said nothing but pointed up the stairs towards where his wife was standing. Now that the hall door was closed the voice and the piano could be heard more clearly. Gabriel held up his hand for them to be silent. The song seemed to be in the old Irish tonality and the singer seemed uncertain both of his words and of his voice. The voice, made plaintive by distance and by the singer's hoarseness, faintly illuminated the cadence of the air with words expressing grief:

O, the rain falls on my heavy locks
And the dew wets my skin,
My babe lies cold …

—O, exclaimed Mary Jane. It's Bartell D'Arcy singing and he wouldn't sing all the night. O, I'll get him to sing a song before he goes.

—O, do, Mary Jane, said Aunt Kate.

Mary Jane brushed past the others and ran to the staircase, but before she reached it the singing stopped and the piano was closed abruptly.

—O, what a pity! she cried. Is he coming down, Gretta?

Gabriel heard his wife answer yes and saw her come down towards them. A few steps behind her were Mr. Bartell D'Arcy and Miss O'Callaghan.

—O, Mr. D'Arcy, cried Mary Jane, it's downright mean of you to break off like that when we were all in raptures listening to you.

—I have been at him all the evening, said Miss O'Callaghan, and Mrs. Conroy, too, and he told us he had a dreadful cold and couldn't sing.

—O, Mr. D'Arcy, said Aunt Kate, now that was a great fib to tell.

—Can't you see that I'm as hoarse as a crow? said Mr. D'Arcy roughly.

He went into the pantry hastily and put on his overcoat. The others, taken aback by his rude speech, could find nothing to say. Aunt Kate wrinkled her brows and made signs to the others to drop the subject. Mr. D'Arcy stood swathing his neck carefully and frowning.

—It's the weather, said Aunt Julia, after a pause.

—Yes, everybody has colds, said Aunt Kate readily, everybody.

—They say, said Mary Jane, we haven't had snow like it for thirty years; and I read this morning in the newspapers that the snow is general all over Ireland.

—I love the look of snow, said Aunt Julia sadly.

—So do I, said Miss O'Callaghan. I think Christmas is never really Christmas unless we have the snow on the ground.

—But poor Mr. D'Arcy doesn't like the snow, said Aunt Kate, smiling.

Mr. D'Arcy came from the pantry, fully swathed and buttoned, and in a repentant tone told them the history of his cold. Everyone gave him advice and said it was a great pity and urged him to be very careful of his throat in the night air. Gabriel watched his wife, who did not join in the conversation. She was standing right under the dusty fanlight and the flame of the gas lit up the rich bronze of her hair, which he had seen her drying at the fire a few days before. She was in the same attitude and seemed unaware of the talk about her. At last she turned towards them and Gabriel saw that there was colour on her cheeks and that her eyes were shining. A sudden tide of joy went leaping out of his heart.

—Mr. D'Arcy, she said, what is the name of that song you were singing?

—It's called "The Lass of Aughrim," said Mr. D'Arcy, but I couldn't remember it properly. Why? Do you know it?

—"The Lass of Aughrim," she repeated. I couldn't think of the name.

—It's a very nice air, said Mary Jane. I'm sorry you were not in voice tonight.

—Now, Mary Jane, said Aunt Kate, don't annoy Mr. D'Arcy. I won't have him annoyed.

Seeing that all were ready to start she shepherded them to the door, where good night was said:

—Well, good night, Aunt Kate, and thanks for the pleasant evening.

—Good night, Gabriel. Good-night, Gretta!

—Good night, Aunt Kate, and thanks ever so much. Good night, Aunt Julia.

—O, good night, Gretta, I didn't see you.

—Good night, Mr. D'Arcy. Good night, Miss O'Callaghan.

—Good night, Miss Morkan.

—Good night, again.

—Good night, all. Safe home.

—Good night. Good night.

The morning was still dark. A dull, yellow light brooded over the houses and the river; and the sky seemed to be descending. It was slushy underfoot; and only streaks and patches of snow lay on the roofs, on the parapets of the quay and on the area railings. The lamps were still burning redly in the murky air and, across the river, the palace of the Four Courts stood out menacingly against the heavy sky.

She was walking on before him with Mr. Bartell D'Arcy, her shoes in a brown parcel tucked under one arm and her hands holding her skirt up from the slush. She had no longer any grace of attitude, but Gabriel's eyes were still bright with happiness. The blood went bounding along his veins; and the thoughts went rioting through his brain, proud, joyful, tender, valorous.

She was walking on before him so lightly and so erect that he longed to run after her noiselessly, catch her by the shoulders and say something foolish and affectionate into her ear. She seemed to him so frail that he longed to defend her against something and then to be alone with her. Moments of their secret life together burst like stars upon his memory. A heliotrope envelope was lying beside his breakfast cup and he was caressing it with his hand. Birds were twittering in the ivy and the sunny web of the curtain was shimmering along the floor: he could not eat for happiness. They were standing on the crowded platform and he was placing a ticket inside the warm palm of her glove. He was standing with her in the cold, looking in through a grated window at a man making bottles in a roaring furnace. It was very cold. Her face, fragrant in the cold air, was quite close to his; and suddenly he called out to the man at the furnace:

—Is the fire hot, sir?

But the man could not hear with the noise of the furnace. It was just as well. He might have answered rudely.

A wave of yet more tender joy escaped from his heart and went coursing in warm flood along his arteries. Like the tender fire of stars moments of their life together, that no one knew of or would ever know of, broke upon and illumined his memory. He longed to recall to her those moments, to make her forget the years of their dull existence together and remember only their moments of ecstasy. For the years, he felt, had not quenched his soul or hers. Their children, his writing, her household cares had not quenched all their souls' tender fire. In one letter that he had written to her then he had said: *Why is it that words like these seem to me so dull and cold? Is it because there is no word tender enough to be your name?*

Like distant music these words that he had written years before were borne towards him from the past. He longed to be alone with her. When the others had gone away, when he and she were in the room in the hotel, then they would be alone together. He would call her softly:

—Gretta!

Perhaps she would not hear at once: she would be undressing. Then something in his voice would strike her. She would turn and look at him ...

At the corner of Winetavern Street they met a cab. He was glad of its rattling noise as it saved him from conversation. She was looking out of the window and seemed tired. The others spoke only a few words, pointing out some building or street. The horse galloped along wearily under the murky morning sky, dragging his old rattling box after his heels, and Gabriel was again in a cab with her, galloping to catch the boat, galloping to their honeymoon.

As the cab drove across O'Connell Bridge Miss O'Callaghan said:

—They say you never cross O'Connell Bridge without seeing a white horse.

—I see a white man this time, said Gabriel.

—Where? asked Mr. Bartell D'Arcy.

Gabriel pointed to the statue, on which lay patches of snow. Then he nodded familiarly to it and waved his hand.

—Good night, Dan, he said gaily.

When the cab drew up before the hotel, Gabriel jumped out and, in spite of Mr. Bartell D'Arcy's protest, paid the driver. He gave the man a shilling over his fare. The man saluted and said:

—A prosperous New Year to you, sir.

—The same to you, said Gabriel cordially.

She leaned for a moment on his arm in getting out of the cab and while standing at the curbstone, bidding the others good night. She leaned lightly on his arm, as lightly as when she had danced with him a few hours before. He had felt proud and happy then, happy that she was his, proud of her grace and wifely carriage. But now, after the kindling again of so many memories, the first touch of her body, musical and strange and perfumed, sent through him a keen pang of lust. Under cover of her silence he pressed her arm closely to his side; and, as they stood at the hotel door, he felt that they had escaped from their lives and duties, escaped from home and friends and run away together with wild and radiant hearts to a new adventure.

An old man was dozing in a great hooded chair in the hall. He lit a candle in the office and went before them to the stairs. They followed him in silence, their feet falling in soft thuds on the thickly carpeted stairs. She mounted the stairs behind the porter, her head bowed in the ascent, her frail shoulders curved as with a burden, her skirt girt tightly about her. He could have flung his arms about her hips and held her still, for his arms were trembling with desire to seize her and only the stress of his nails against the palms of his hands held the wild impulse of his body in check. The porter halted on the stairs to settle his guttering candle. They halted, too, on the steps below him. In the silence Gabriel could hear the falling of the molten wax into the tray and the thumping of his own heart against his ribs.

The porter led them along a corridor and opened a door. Then he set his unstable candle down on a toilet-table and asked at what hour they were to be called in the morning.

—Eight, said Gabriel.

The porter pointed to the tap of the electric light and began a muttered apology, but Gabriel cut him short.

—We don't want any light. We have light enough from the street. And I say, he added, pointing to the candle, you might remove that handsome article, like a good man.

The porter took up his candle again, but slowly, for he was surprised by such a novel idea. Then he mumbled good night and went out. Gabriel shot the lock to.

A ghastly light from the streetlamp lay in a long shaft from one window to the door. Gabriel threw his overcoat and hat on a couch and crossed the room towards the window. He looked down into the street in order that his emotion might calm a little. Then he turned and leaned against a chest of drawers with his back to the light. She had taken off her hat and cloak and was standing before a large swinging mirror, unhooking her waist. Gabriel paused for a few moments, watching her, and then said:

—Gretta!

She turned away from the mirror slowly and walked along the shaft of light towards him. Her face looked so serious and weary that the words would not pass Gabriel's lips. No, it was not the moment yet.

—You looked tired, he said.

—I am a little, she answered.

—You don't feel ill or weak?

—No, tired: that's all.

She went on to the window and stood there, looking out. Gabriel waited again and then, fearing that diffidence was about to conquer him, he said abruptly:

—By the way, Gretta!

—What is it?

—You know that poor fellow Malins? he said quickly.

—Yes. What about him?

—Well, poor fellow, he's a decent sort of chap, after all, continued Gabriel in a false voice. He gave me back that sovereign I lent him, and I didn't expect it, really. It's a pity he wouldn't keep away from that Browne, because he's not a bad fellow, really.

He was trembling now with annoyance. Why did she seem so abstracted? He did not know how he could begin. Was she annoyed, too, about something? If she would only turn to him or come to him of her own accord! To take her as she was would be brutal. No, he must see some ardour in her eyes first. He longed to be master of her strange mood.

—When did you lend him the pound? she asked, after a pause.

Gabriel strove to restrain himself from breaking out into brutal language about the sottish Malins and his pound. He longed to cry to her from his soul, to crush her body against his, to overmaster her. But he said:

—O, at Christmas, when he opened that little Christmas-card shop in Henry Street.

He was in such a fever of rage and desire that he did not hear her come from the window. She stood before him for an instant, looking at him strangely. Then, suddenly raising herself on tiptoe and resting her hands lightly on his shoulders, she kissed him.

—You are a very generous person, Gabriel, she said.

Gabriel, trembling with delight at her sudden kiss and at the quaintness of her phrase, put his hands on her hair and began smoothing it back, scarcely touching it with his fingers. The washing had made it fine and brilliant. His heart was brimming over with happiness. Just when he was wishing for it she had come to him of her own accord. Perhaps her thoughts had been running with his. Perhaps she had felt the impetuous desire that was in him, and then the yielding mood had come upon her. Now that she had fallen to him so easily, he wondered why he had been so diffident.

He stood, holding her head between his hands. Then, slipping one arm swiftly about her body and drawing her towards him, he said softly:

—Gretta, dear, what are you thinking about?

She did not answer nor yield wholly to his arm. He said again, softly:

—Tell me what it is, Gretta. I think I know what is the matter. Do I know?

She did not answer at once. Then she said in an outburst of tears:

—O, I am thinking about that song, "The Lass of Aughrim."

She broke loose from him and ran to the bed and, throwing her arms across the bed-rail, hid her face. Gabriel stood stock-still for a moment in astonishment and then followed her. As he passed in the way of the cheval glass he caught sight of himself in full length, his broad, well-filled shirt front, the face whose expression always puzzled him when he saw it in a mirror, and his glimmering gilt-rimmed eyeglasses. He halted a few paces from her and said:

—What about the song? Why does that make you cry?

She raised her head from her arms and dried her eyes with the back of her hand like a child. A kinder note than he had intended went into his voice.

—Why, Gretta? he asked.

—I am thinking about a person long ago who used to sing that song.

—And who was the person long ago? asked Gabriel, smiling.

—It was a person I used to know in Galway when I was living with my grandmother, she said.

The smile passed away from Gabriel's face. A dull anger began to gather again at the back of his mind and the dull fires of his lust began to glow angrily in his veins.

—Someone you were in love with? he asked ironically.

—It was a young boy I used to know, she answered, named Michael Furey. He used to sing that song, "The Lass of Aughrim." He was very delicate.

Gabriel was silent. He did not wish her to think that he was interested in this delicate boy.

—I can see him so plainly, she said, after a moment. Such eyes as he had: big, dark eyes! And such an expression in them—an expression!

—O, then, you are in love with him? said Gabriel.

—I used to go out walking with him, she said, when I was in Galway.

A thought flew across Gabriel's mind.

—Perhaps that was why you wanted to go to Galway with that Ivors girl? he said coldly.

She looked at him and asked in surprise:

—What for?

Her eyes made Gabriel feel awkward. He shrugged his shoulders and said:

—How do I know? To see him, perhaps.

She looked away from him along the shaft of light towards the window in silence.

—He is dead, she said at length. He died when he was only seventeen. Isn't it a terrible thing to die so young as that?

—What was he? asked Gabriel, still ironically.

—He was in the gasworks, she said.

Gabriel felt humiliated by the failure of his irony and by the evocation of this figure from the dead, a boy in the gasworks. While he had been full of memories of their secret life together, full of tenderness and joy and desire, she had been comparing him in her mind with another. A shameful consciousness of his own person assailed him. He saw himself as a ludicrous figure, acting as a pennyboy for his aunts, a nervous, well-meaning sentimentalist, orating to vulgarians and idealising his own clownish lusts, the pitiable fatuous fellow he had caught a glimpse of in the mirror. Instinctively he turned his back more to the light lest she might see the shame that burned upon his forehead.

He tried to keep up his tone of cold interrogation, but his voice when he spoke was humble and indifferent.

—I suppose you were in love with this Michael Furey, Gretta, he said.

—I was great with him at that time, she said.

Her voice was veiled and sad. Gabriel, feeling now how vain it would be to try to lead her whither he had purposed, caressed one of her hands and said, also sadly:

—And what did he die of so young, Gretta? Consumption, was it?

—I think he died for me, she answered.

A vague terror seized Gabriel at this answer, as if, at that hour when he had hoped to triumph, some impalpable and vindictive being was coming against him, gathering forces against him in its vague world. But he shook himself free of it with an effort of reason and continued to caress her hand. He did not question her again, for he felt that she would tell him of herself. Her hand was warm and moist: it did not respond to his touch, but he continued to caress it just as he had caressed her first letter to him that spring morning.

—It was in the winter, she said, about the beginning of the winter when I was going to leave my grandmother's and come up here to the convent. And he was ill at the time in his lodgings in Galway and wouldn't be let out, and his people in Oughterard were written to. He was in decline, they said, or something like that. I never knew rightly.

She paused for a moment and sighed.

—Poor fellow, she said. He was very fond of me and he was such a gentle boy. We used to go out together, walking, you know, Gabriel, like the way they do in the country. He was going to study singing only for his health. He had a very good voice, poor Michael Furey.

—Well; and then? asked Gabriel.

—And then when it came to the time for me to leave Galway and come up to the convent he was much worse and I wouldn't be let see him so I wrote him a letter saying I was going up to Dublin and would be back in the summer, and hoping he would be better then.

She paused for a moment to get her voice under control, and then went on:

—Then the night before I left, I was in my grandmother's house in Nuns' Island, packing up, and I heard gravel thrown up against the window. The window was so wet I couldn't see, so I ran downstairs as I was and slipped out the back into the garden and there was the poor fellow at the end of the garden, shivering.

—And did you not tell him to go back? asked Gabriel.

—I implored of him to go home at once and told him he would get his death in the rain. But he said he did not want to live. I can see his eyes as well as well! He was standing at the end of the wall where there was a tree.

—And did he go home? asked Gabriel.

—Yes, he went home. And when I was only a week in the convent he died and he was buried in Oughterard, where his people came from. O, the day I heard that, that he was dead!

She stopped, choking with sobs, and, overcome by emotion, flung herself face downward on the bed, sobbing in the quilt. Gabriel held her hand for a moment longer, irresolutely, and then, shy of intruding on her grief, let it fall gently and walked quietly to the window.

She was fast asleep.

Gabriel, leaning on his elbow, looked for a few moments unresentfully on her tangled hair and half-open mouth, listening to her deep-drawn breath. So she had had that romance in her life: a man had died for her sake. It hardly pained him now to think how poor a part he, her husband, had played in her life. He watched her while she slept, as though he and she had never lived together as man and wife. His curious eyes rested long upon her face and on her hair: and, as he thought of what she must have been then, in that time of her first girlish beauty, a strange, friendly pity for her entered his soul. He did not like to say even to himself that her face was no longer beautiful, but he knew that it was no longer the face for which Michael Furey had braved death.

Perhaps she had not told him all the story. His eyes moved to the chair over which she had thrown some of her clothes. A petticoat string dangled to the floor. One boot stood upright, its limp upper fallen down: the fellow of it lay upon its side. He wondered at his riot of emotions of an hour before. From what had it proceeded? From his aunt's supper, from his own foolish speech, from the wine and dancing, the merrymaking when saying good-night in the hall, the pleasure of the walk along the river in the snow. Poor Aunt Julia! She, too, would soon be a shade with the shade of Patrick Morkan and his horse. He had caught that haggard look upon her face for a moment when she was singing "Arrayed for the Bridal." Soon, perhaps, he would be sitting in that same drawing room, dressed in black, his silk hat on his knees. The blinds would be drawn down and Aunt Kate would be sitting beside him, crying and blowing her nose and telling him how Julia had died. He would cast about in his mind for some words that might console her, and would find only lame and useless ones. Yes, yes: that would happen very soon.

The air of the room chilled his shoulders. He stretched himself cautiously along under the sheets and lay down beside his wife. One by one, they were all becoming shades. Better pass boldly into that other world, in the full glory of some passion, than fade and wither dismally with age. He thought of how she who lay beside him had locked in her heart for so many years that image of her lover's eyes when he had told her that he did not wish to live.

Generous tears filled Gabriel's eyes. He had never felt like that himself towards any woman, but he knew that such a feeling must be love. The tears gathered more thickly in his eyes and in the partial darkness he imagined he saw the form of a young man standing under a dripping tree. Other forms were near. His soul had approached that region where dwell the vast hosts of the dead. He was conscious of, but could not apprehend, their wayward and flickering existence. His own identity was fading out into a grey impalpable world: the solid world itself, which these dead had one time reared and lived in, was dissolving and dwindling.

A few light taps upon the pane made him turn to the window. It had begun to snow again. He watched sleepily the flakes, silver and dark, falling obliquely against the lamplight. The time had come for him to set out on his journey westward. Yes, the newspapers were right: snow was general all over Ireland. It was falling on every part of the dark central plain, on the treeless hills, falling softly upon the Bog of Allen and, farther westward, softly falling into the dark mutinous Shannon waves. It was falling, too, upon every part of the lonely churchyard on the hill where Michael Furey lay buried. It lay thickly drifted on the crooked crosses and headstones, on the spears of the little gate, on the barren thorns. His soul swooned slowly as he heard the snow falling faintly through the universe and faintly falling, like the descent of their last end, upon all the living and the dead.

ELIZABETH BOWEN (1899–1973) was the author of ten novels and eight collections of short stories, the genre in which she felt most comfortable. Bowen's tragic childhood brought her from Ireland to Hythe, England, where she stayed for most of her life. She regularly traveled between the two islands, reporting on wartime Ireland for the Ministry of Information and visiting her ancestral home in County Cork, the history of which she described in her first nonfiction book, *Bowen's Court.*

FRANCES BROWNE (1816–1879) was known as the "Blind Poetess of Donegal," having lost her sight as a result of smallpox as an infant. She is best remembered for her widely-translated 1856 collection of children's stories, *Granny's Wonderful Chair and the Stories It Told*, but also published short stories, poems, and an autobiography, *My Share of the World*, in 1862.

ANNE ENRIGHT (1962–) has published seven novels and three short-story collections, along with one nonfiction book, *Making Babies: Stumbling into Motherhood* (2004). Before focusing on writing she was a producer and director on the groundbreaking Irish television series *Nighthawks*. Enright's novel *The Gathering* won the 2007 Booker Prize, and she was named the inaugural Laureate for Irish Fiction in 2015.

JAMES JOYCE (1882–1941) became one of the most influential authors of the twentieth century with just four books of fiction, including the modernist masterpiece *Ulysses* (1922), along with two poetry collections and a play, *Exiles* (1918). Joyce's early life, described in *A Portrait of the Artist as a Young Man* (1916), sunk rapidly from luxury to relative squalor. Though he left Dublin in 1902 for a series of European cities, only returning three times between 1904 and 1912, his fiction was never set anywhere else.

CLAIRE KEEGAN (1968–) is a short story writer and creative writing teacher. Her debut collection, *Antarctica*, won the inaugural William Trevor Prize, and her story "Foster" won the prestigious Davy Byrnes Award, selected by American novelist Richard Ford. Keegan has taught at Villanova University, Trinity College Dublin, and Pembroke College Cambridge.

BERNARD MacLAVERTY (1942–) is a northern Irish novelist and short story writer. After ten years as a medical laboratory technician in Belfast, he studied at Queen's University Belfast and then moved with his family to Scotland, where he still lives. He has published five novels, two of which—*Cal* (1983) and *Lamb* (1980)—he adapted for the screen. He has also published five books of short stories, television and radio plays, and children's books.

AISLING MAGUIRE (1958–) earned a PhD from the National University of Ireland in Dublin with a thesis on the poetry of Ted Hughes and Seamus Heaney. She has written two novels; contributed short stories, book reviews, and features to a variety of anthologies, Irish and international publications, and RTÉ 1; and previously worked as a parliamentary reporter in the Houses of the Oireachtas.

MÁIRE MHAC a tSAOI (1922–) is an Irish-language poet who spent her childhood between Dublin and the Irish-speaking region of Kerry, before studying at University College Dublin and the Sorbonne. She has published several volumes of Irish-language poetry, as well as critical essays and a nonfiction book, *Concise History of Ireland* (1972), written with her husband, Conor Cruise O'Brien.

KATHERINE FRANCES (K. F.) PURDON (1852–1918) was a novelist, short story writer, essayist, and poet from County Meath. Her fiction is written mostly in a Hiberno-English dialect. She was connected to the Irish Revival movement, with her writing often illustrated by Jack B. Yeats, and her story "Candle and Crib" performed as a play at the Abbey Theatre in 1918. She was a founding member of the United Irishwomen, now known as the Irish Countrywomen's Association.

PATRICK AUGUSTINE (CANON) SHEEHAN (1852–1913) was born in County Cork and became parish priest of Doneraile, County Cork, in 1894. As a priest, he began writing novels, essays, and poems, alongside his sermons. All of his writing was part of the same project of preserving traditional Catholic values in response to rapid modernization in Ireland. He published ten novels in his lifetime, as well as the 1905 collection *A Spoiled Priest and Other Stories*, and a posthumous collection of his poetry was published in 1921.

COLM TÓIBÍN (1955–) is an award-winning novelist, short story writer, and journalist from Enniscorthy, County Wexford. He was educated at University College Dublin and has taught creative writing and literature at such institutions as Stanford University, Princeton University, and the University of Manchester. The film adaptation of his 2009 novel *Brooklyn* was nominated for Best Picture at the 2015 Academy Awards.

WILLIAM TREVOR (1928–2016) began his career as a sculptor and art teacher in Northern Ireland and England, but became a full-time writer at the age of thirty-six, after the critical success of his second novel, *The Old Boys* (1964). Throughout his life he published a total of twenty novels and almost one hundred stories, for which he was especially acclaimed, with critics highlighting his straightforward style and attention to the everyday.

THE WEXFORD or ENNISCORTHY CAROL is one of thirteen carols from the Kilmore Carols, a cycle of carols from south county Wexford. It was passed down orally, though probably for only a few centuries, before being transcribed by William Henry Grattan Flood in the 1928 *Oxford Book of Carols*. Wexford was one of the few historically English-speaking counties in Ireland, and "The Wexford Carol" was written originally in English, though it has been translated into Irish.

WILLIAM BUTLER (W. B.) YEATS (1865–1939) was a central force behind the Irish Revival in literature as the founder of the Abbey Theatre in Dublin. He was a significant dramatist, but is best known for his poems, such as "The Second Coming" and "The Lake Isle of Innisfree," which are among the most beloved and respected in Irish literature. He was awarded the Nobel Prize in Literature in 1923, the first of four Irish laureates.

A VERY GERMAN CHRISTMAS

This collection brings together traditional and contemporary holiday stories from Austria, Switzerland and Germany. You'll find classic works by the Brothers Grimm, Johann Wolfgang von Goethe, Heinrich Heine, Thomas Mann, Rainer Maria Rilke, Hermann Hesse, Joseph Roth and Arthur Schnitzler, as well as more recent tales by writers like Heinrich Böll, Peter Stamm and Martin Suter.

A VERY SCANDINAVIAN CHRISTMAS

The best Scandinavian holiday stories including classics by Hans Christian Andersen, Nobel Prize winner Selma Lagerlöf, August Strindberg as well as popular Norwegian author Karl Ove Knausgaard. These Nordic tales—coming from the very region where much traditional Christmas imagery originates—convey a festive spirit laden with lingonberries, elks, gnomes and aquavit in abundance. A smorgasbord of unexpected literary gifts sure to provide plenty of pleasure and *hygge*, that specifically Scandinavian blend of coziness and contentment.

A VERY FRENCH CHRISTMAS

A continuation of the very popular Very Christmas Series, this collection brings together the best French Christmas stories of all time in an elegant and vibrant collection featuring classics by Guy de Maupassant and Alphonse Daudet, plus stories by the esteemed twentieth century author Irène Némirovsky and contemporary writers Dominique Fabre and Jean-Philippe Blondel. With a holiday spirit conveyed through sparkling Paris streets, opulent feasts, wandering orphans, flickering desire, and more than a little wine, this collection proves that the French have mastered Christmas.

A VERY ITALIAN CHRISTMAS

This volume brings together the best Italian Christmas stories of all time in a fascinating collection featuring classic tales and contemporary works. With writing that dates from the Renaissance to the present day, from Boccaccio to Pirandello, as well as Anna Maria Ortese, Natalia Ginzburg and Nobel laureate Grazia Deledda, this choice selection delights and intrigues. Like everything the Italians do, this is Christmas with its very own verve and flair, the perfect literary complement to a *Buon Natale italiano*.

A VERY RUSSIAN CHRISTMAS
This is Russian Christmas celebrated in supreme pleasure and pain by the greatest of writers, from Dostoevsky and Tolstoy to Chekhov and Teffi. The dozen stories in this collection will satisfy every reader, and with their wit, humor, and tenderness, packed full of sentimental songs, footmen, whirling winds, solitary nights, snow drifts, and hopeful children, the collection proves that Nobody Does Christmas Like the Russians.

THE EYE by Philippe Costamagna
It's a rare and secret profession, comprising a few dozen people around the world equipped with a mysterious mixture of knowledge and innate sensibility. Summoned to Swiss bank vaults, Fifth Avenue apartments, and Tokyo storerooms, they are entrusted by collectors, dealers, and museums to decide if a coveted picture is real or fake and to determine if it was painted by Leonardo da Vinci or Raphael. *The Eye* lifts the veil on the rarified world of connoisseurs devoted to the authentication and discovery of Old Master artworks.

WHAT'S LEFT OF THE NIGHT by Ersi Sotiropoulos
Constantine Cavafy arrives in Paris in 1897 on a trip that will deeply shape his future and push him toward his poetic inclination. With this lyrical novel, tinged with an hallucinatory eroticism that unfolds over three unforgettable days, celebrated Greek author Ersi Sotiropoulos depicts Cavafy in the midst of a journey of self-discovery across a continent on the brink of massive change. A stunning portrait of a budding author—before he became C.P. Cavafy, one of the 20th century's greatest poets—that illuminates the complex relationship of art, life, and the erotic desires that trigger creativity.

THE ANIMAL GAZER by Edgardo Franzosini
A hypnotic novel inspired by the strange and fascinating life of sculptor Rembrandt Bugatti, brother of the fabled automaker. Bugatti obsessively observes and sculpts the baboons, giraffes, and panthers in European zoos, finding empathy with their plight and identifying with their life in captivity. Rembrandt Bugatti's work, now being rediscovered, is displayed in major art museums around the world and routinely fetches large sums at auction. Edgardo Franzosini recreates the young artist's life with intense lyricism, passion, and sensitivity.

ALLMEN AND THE DRAGONFLIES by Martin Suter

Johann Friedrich von Allmen has exhausted his family fortune by living in Old World grandeur despite present-day financial constraints. Forced to downscale, Allmen inhabits the garden house of his former Zurich estate, attended by his Guatemalan butler, Carlos. This is the first of a series of humorous, fast-paced detective novels devoted to a memorable gentleman thief. A thrilling art heist escapade infused with European high culture and luxury that doesn't shy away from the darker side of human nature.

THE MADELEINE PROJECT by Clara Beaudoux

A young woman moves into a Paris apartment and discovers a storage room filled with the belongings of the previous owner, a certain Madeleine who died in her late nineties, and whose treasured possessions nobody seems to want. In an audacious act of journalism driven by personal curiosity and humane tenderness, Clara Beaudoux embarks on *The Madeleine Project*, documenting what she finds on Twitter with text and photographs, introducing the world to an unsung 20th century figure.

ADUA by Igiaba Scego

Adua, an immigrant from Somalia to Italy, has lived in Rome for nearly forty years. She came seeking freedom from a strict father and an oppressive regime, but her dreams of film stardom ended in shame. Now that the civil war in Somalia is over, her homeland calls her. She must decide whether to return and reclaim her inheritance, but also how to take charge of her own story and build a future.

IF VENICE DIES by Salvatore Settis

Internationally renowned art historian Salvatore Settis ignites a new debate about the Pearl of the Adriatic and cultural patrimony at large. In this fiery blend of history and cultural analysis, Settis argues that "hit-and-run" visitors are turning Venice and other landmark urban settings into shopping malls and theme parks. This is a passionate plea to secure the soul of Venice, written with consummate authority, wide-ranging erudition and élan.

THE MADONNA OF NOTRE DAME by Alexis Ragougneau
Fifty thousand people jam into Notre Dame Cathedral to celebrate the Feast of the Assumption. The next morning, a beautiful young woman clothed in white kneels at prayer in a cathedral side chapel. But when someone accidentally bumps against her, her body collapses. She has been murdered. This thrilling novel illuminates shadowy corners of the world's most famous cathedral, shedding light on good and evil with suspense, compassion and wry humor.

THE YEAR OF THE COMET by Sergei Lebedev
A story of a Russian boyhood and coming of age as the Soviet Union is on the brink of collapse. Lebedev depicts a vast empire coming apart at the seams, transforming a very public moment into something tender and personal, and writes with stunning beauty and shattering insight about childhood and the growing consciousness of a boy in the world.

THE LAST WEYNFELDT by Martin Suter
Adrian Weynfeldt is an art expert in an international auction house, a bachelor in his mid-fifties living in a grand Zurich apartment filled with costly paintings and antiques. Always correct and well-mannered, he's given up on love until one night—entirely out of character for him—Weynfeldt decides to take home a ravishing but unaccountable young woman and gets embroiled in an art forgery scheme that threatens his buttoned up existence. This refined page-turner moves behind elegant bourgeois facades into darker recesses of the heart.

THE LAST SUPPER by Klaus Wivel
Alarmed by the oppression of 7.5 million Christians in the Middle East, journalist Klaus Wivel traveled to Iraq, Lebanon, Egypt, and the Palestinian territories to learn about their fate. He found a minority under threat of death and humiliation, desperate in the face of rising Islamic extremism and without hope their situation will improve. An unsettling account of a severely beleaguered religious group living, so it seems, on borrowed time. Wivel asks, Why have we not done more to protect these people?

To purchase these titles and for more information please visit newvesselpress.com.